W9-ATY-006

Trusting Fate

Tamra Lassiter

www.tamra.lassiter.com

Trusting Fate

Tamra Lassiter

This is a work of fiction. Certain real locations are mentioned, however all names, characters, events and incidents described in this book are fictitious or a product of the author's imagination. Any resemblance to real persons, living or deceased, is entirely coincidental.

TRUSTING FATE

Copyright © 2016 by Tamra Lassiter

All rights reserved.

ISBN-13: 978-1-942235-80-4(trade paperback)
ISBN-13: 978-1-942235-81-1(e-book)

www.tamralassiter.com

For Rhonda

Chapter One

Brady

Just add this rain to my list of problems. Five days until Christmas, and instead of feeling jolly, I'm leaning much more towards bah humbug. Rhonda's timing sucks, not that she can pick when she has to have an emergency appendectomy, but geez, couldn't the surgery be any other time? The Mayfair staff is spread thin over the next couple weeks, and the holidays are likely to be our busiest time.

The rain pounds against the awning of the restaurant we've worked so hard to create. Meg's been a highly successful business partner and chef. Mayfair has become the place to go for special occasions and has enjoyed more success in its first six months than I ever imagined. I know we'll get through this, but how? It wasn't easy to find capable fine-dining staff in Davidson, Virginia in the first place. Our new hires required a lot of specialized training. Our guests have grown accustomed to a certain level of service. We can't let them down.

The rumbling sound of a Harley wakes me from my thoughts. The Dyna Glide makes its way down Main Street. Nice bike for sure, but today is not the kind of day to ride a motorcycle. What the hell is he thinking, riding in this downpour?

The front tire bucks. The rider recovers. Maybe that little move will make him think better of being out here. Ridicul...My brain doesn't finish the thought because the bike is now sliding down the wet street into oncoming traffic.

Shit. Mom's car barrels towards it.

The rider stops only a few feet from the bumper of my mother's Avalon. Thank the Lord, Mom was able to brake in time to avoid hitting the motorcyclist. I drop my umbrella and briefcase onto the sidewalk and rush into the street and then stop. Who do I go to first? Mom will be beside herself. She still sits in her car. I can't make out her facial expression through the heavy rain, but while she'll likely be very upset, she didn't just slide down the street under a motorcycle.

With a renewed sense of purpose, I rush the few remaining steps to the biker. He releases his grip from the handlebars of his bike and lets his head rest on the pavement.

"Dude, are you okay? Let's get your bike off of you."

I kneel down next to the fallen motorcycle and with a grunt, push the bike to a standing position. It's not an easy task. I'm feeling glad the owner didn't go with a Fat Boy or something heavier. This one's heavy enough. I hold the bike in a standing position, move around to the other side, and engage the kick stand. The rain is relentless.

"You poor dear." Mom is with me now. Her short silver hair is already plastered to her head from the pouring rain. She bends over near the rider's head. "Is anything broken?"

A muffled response comes from the rider, who sits up and begins to unstrap his helmet. His movements give me some relief. This could have been so much worse. My own mother could have run over the guy right in front of me.

"Dude, you're one lucky guy."

Not. A. Dude.

Deep brown eyes look back at me, revealing every emotion the rider is feeling. Shock, fear, and relief take their turns skittering across a feminine face.

He's a she.

I can hardly believe the sight before me, but my body keeps hammering the truth home with jolts of electricity that travel straight to my groin, despite the cold rain.

For several long seconds we merely stare at each other. She's not at all gruff like the image I have in my head of a biker chick—although I admit I've never actually known one. She seems soft, not tough. Her light brown hair is pulled back in a ponytail. It's a bit messy from the helmet. She wears no makeup. Her pale cheeks are wet from tears or the rain or both.

Meg arrives with an umbrella, holding it over the woman's head. It's too late for any of us to be dry, but at least she's safe from the pounding drops.

"Do you think you can stand?"

She nods. "I believe so." Her voice reminds me of honey. What a strange thing to think about at this moment. Besides the chaos of being in the middle of the street in the pouring rain, what the heck does honey sound like?

The wisps of hair that have escaped the hair band are now plastered against her cheeks. She shivers.

"Let me help you."

I extend my hand. She removes her leather riding gloves and places her hand in mine. The touch of her skin sends a shock all the way up my arm. I forcibly close my mouth. Did that really just happen? One look into those wide, coffee-colored eyes, and I know I'm not the only one who felt that jolt. What the hell?

Maybe there's too much adrenaline pumping through us both right now. I can't be attracted to someone from merely a touch, especially a woman decked out from head to toe in leather biker clothes. This woman is not my style. At all.

She gives her head a shake. She's rattled just as much by this nonsense as I am.

Regardless of what is making me temporarily unstable, I pull her to her feet. She's light as a feather, and it's no wonder since she's thin and appears to be only a few inches over five feet tall. Once standing, she takes an unsteady step to try out her injured leg and frowns.

"Let me help."

Without waiting for a response, I lift her up into my arms. She squeals but doesn't protest. Meg adjusts the umbrella as best as she can to cover the two of us together. It's a nice gesture, but it hardly matters as we're both completely soaked. Maybe the biker woman's leathers protected her from the rain, but my puffy winter coat has already soaked through.

The woman shivers in my arms. I pull her tighter to me. There's still no protest. I take a deep breath, and my lungs are filled with the scent of honeysuckle.

Honeysuckle. Is that what biker chicks smell like? Who knew? I would have thought it would be something more earthy, although I don't know why. They're women. She's a woman. I can still hardly believe it.

I steal another look at her. Her skin is a creamy

white down the bridge of her thin nose but rosy on her cheeks—whether from the cold or the embarrassment of the last few moments. Her eyelids flutter closed, highlighting long, thick eyelashes the same dark brown color as her eyes.

I step onto the sidewalk and set her down underneath the Mayfair awning where I was standing when I first saw her. Of course, I thought it was a guy on the motorcycle, and I was wondering what on earth he was doing riding in this weather. Now that I know *he* is actually a *she*, it seems even more insane. I'm not sexist, only more protective of women. I have a younger sister whom I've always looked out for, and this kind of situation always makes me think of Kate.

Kate comes forward now, out of the crowd of onlookers, and approaches Mom.

"What happened?"

"I almost hit this poor woman. Thank goodness I was able to stop in time." Mom turns to the biker chick. "You poor dear. We need to call 9-1-1."

"I already did," Meg announces. "Grace, why don't you come inside and sit down."

I take a good look at Mom for the first time since seeing her almost hit the biker. Her skin is pale white. It's difficult to tell if it's the shock of what just happened or what she's been going through with her cancer. It may be a bit of both.

"That's a good idea." I open the front door. "Why don't you both come in and sit down?"

"Absolutely not. I'm drenched to the bone, and I don't want to ruin any of your beautiful upholstery."

"I am perfectly fine to stand as well." Her voice hitches. She should most definitely sit down. Before I can argue with either of them, the sound of the siren cuts through the din of the pounding rain.

The ambulance weaves its way through the traffic. Fortunately, it's coming from the south where the lane is clear. The north side is blocked by the motorcycle and Mom's Toyota, which is still idling in the middle of the street. Cars are lined up behind her and all the way down Main Street. This is the most traffic, and likely the most excitement, these people will see all year.

We watch as my brother-in-law, Hunter, who's also a town policeman, takes a few photos of the scene. He's getting soaked as well, but at least he's wearing proper rain gear over his uniform.

Tyler, another of Davidson's finest, and my business partner Meg's husband, approaches our little group. "Everyone okay here?"

We all look at the mystery woman. She stands just about two feet from me, her arms hugged to her. She shivers.

"You poor thing," Mom says before stepping to her and wrapping her arm around the woman's shoulders. "What's your name, sweetie?"

"Vivienne," she says with another shiver. "P-please call me V-Viv."

"I'm Grace Richardson. This is my son, Brady."

Mom gestures to me. My eyes meet Vivienne's and lock. "And this is my daughter, Kate. Her husband, Hunter, is that handsome policeman over there." Vivienne breaks eye contact with me to look at Kate and then Hunter.

"It's very nice to meet you." Vivienne gets all the words out without issue.

Mom hugs Vivienne tighter as the ambulance stops in front of us, blocking the open side of the roadway. Matt Foster, one of our town EMTs, exits the vehicle along with another guy I don't know. They exchange greetings with Hunter, who points in our direction. Hunter then walks Vivienne's bike out of the way before sliding into Mom's car and moving it to the side of the street. The traffic jam on that side of the road is now free to move. I lose track of where Hunter goes with the car because the EMTs are with us now.

"I thank you for coming, but I don't require medical attention."

Vivienne speaks the words as a pronouncement as someone would who's used to getting her way. She stands a bit straighter. Her efforts are useless, and her words are lost. Maybe she doesn't need an ambulance, but she most certainly does need to go to the hospital. I'll put her in the car and drive her there myself if I have to.

"Honey, you need to go with them to get checked out. You could have a concussion or a fractured bone. It's best to get it looked at right away, and I couldn't live with myself if something happened to you." Mom adds the stern but concerned expression I've seen so many times in my life.

Vivienne looks as if she's going to argue the point, but she doesn't even open her mouth. Smart woman. Not many people argue with my mom and win.

"Yes, ma'am," she finally concedes.

"I'll ride with you to the hospital."

"Thank you."

"You need to let them take a look at you, too, Mom." Kate speaks the words before I do.

"Me. Why?"

"Because you look pale," Kate answers matter-of-factly.

"And I couldn't live with myself if something happened to you." I try to keep my voice light so as not to completely piss her off. Her unsure expression becomes a scowl. "Seriously, Mom. Please." I place my hand on her arm and squeeze for extra assurance.

"Oh, fine. But this better be quick. I have cookies to decorate."

Chapter Two

Viv

With a big sigh, Mrs. Richardson hugs her children to her in turn. First Brady and then Kate. The brother and sister look very much alike with their pale blue eyes and hair that can only be called red. Brady's hair might be a tad browner when compared to his sister's, but they both look very much alike with their pale, creamy skin and freckles.

Brady's tall—easily a few inches over six feet. He appears to be a combination of both rugged handsomeness and boy-next-door sweetness. Kate is not petite but definitely not a large woman by any means. She just seems capable.

In contrast to her children, Grace is short in

stature and plump with short silver hair and smiling blue eyes. The family resemblance isn't obvious—her complexion is freckle-free and more olive in color than that of her children. Maybe Brady and Kate favor their father.

Thank you, Lord, for letting me stop in time. And Grace Richardson as well. I was a nervous wreck riding in this awful weather in the first place. I was going only as fast as I dared, which in reality was a snail's pace. While I was trying to be hyper-focused on my driving, the road, and the weather, I spent much of the time chastising myself for selecting a motorcycle for this idiotic mission in the first place.

Just because a motorcycle seemed like the best idea for my crazy journey of enlightenment, it was the choice of transportation most unlike anything I'd normally drive, and it would give Grandmother the most shock, I have to admit it was a stupid choice on my part. I have no idea what I'm doing, and I'm too stubborn to admit it out loud. I'm not willing to let anyone know I'm actually still uncomfortable riding this thing despite the fact that I've been on this journey for months.

Someone needs to invent a rain cover for a motorcycle.

Someone has. It's called a car.

Great. Not only have I been alone for so long that I'm beginning to answer my own questions, I'm kind of bitchy about it.

That was the dialogue going through my mind when I lost control. I turned the handlebars in an attempt to get back on course. It was too late. The next thing I knew, I was on the ground, careening toward Grace's car.

I don't think I breathed for a full minute after that. Finally, I laid my head back on the pavement, sucked the cold damp air into my lungs, and tried to not to panic at the fact that I couldn't move the leg that was pinned under my bike. What if I was paralyzed?

So many thoughts rushed through my head at the same time. Because of the charity work we do, my family is acquainted with many doctors and surgeons. Grandmother would call on all of them until she found one who could help me. But what if there was no help?

When I'd opened my eyes, Brady was kneeling beside me.

I held my breath and wiggled my toes. I felt my toes hit the top of my boot.

That started the tears. *Relief*. And I had to get that helmet off my head.

I smelled Brady before I even realized he was with me. The scent of sandalwood filled my being, and I opened my eyes and saw him for the first time. With what seemed like very little effort, he pushed my bike upright.

Brady has barely taken his eyes off of me during this whole ordeal. Even now he's watching the EMT take my blood pressure.

"Your vitals are stable, but we'd still like to take you with us to the hospital to run a few tests. Will you accompany us?"

"I don't think it's necessary for me to ride in the ambulance. The rain is slowing down. I can take my bike to the hospital. Would you please point me in the right direction?"

"I'll give you a ride."

Brady's voice has a gruff quality I haven't heard from him so far. He's clearly declaring that there will be no argument.

"I don't want to impose. You've done so much for me already. "

"It's no imposition. Mom needs to go as well, so you can ride with us."

My eyes catch a glimpse of the growing crowd standing on the sidewalk, dozens of people huddle under umbrellas and the awning for the florist next door. A few are standing out in the rain unprotected, their curiosity stronger than their need to stay dry. They have another thing in common. They each wear a sympathetic expression. I move my gaze from one to the next. A couple of the women give me smiles of encouragement.

I continue to look at one person after another. I can't help but stare at the very last man in the line of about ten people standing closest to us. The man is relatively tall with thinning black hair and dark eyes. His expression isn't sympathetic or encouraging.

Instead, he studies me with an intense gaze as if he's scanning my body for injuries. Goosebumps break out on my arms despite my leather jacket. The man turns and walks away in the opposite direction.

"There's really nothing to think about." My attention moves back to Brady. "You either ride in the ambulance, or you ride with us."

Normally I'd be angry at Brady's demanding tone. Instead, relief hits me hard for the second time today. Truthfully, I would rather get into a car with two almost-strangers than get back on my bike… ever.

After much arguing about where to sit, I settle into the back seat of Brady's minivan. He and Grace were both insistent I sit in the front, but I finally just slid the back door open and got inside. There's no way I'm making that sweet woman climb back here. Grace isn't old by any means—I'd place her around sixty or so, but even with a sore leg, it's easier for me to climb into the back seat.

The ride to the hospital is mostly silent. Grace and I make polite conversation about the weather and the upcoming holidays. We arrive at the hospital with Brady having said nothing.

He pulls right up to the emergency room entrance. Despite the small size of this hospital, they still have valet parking. Brady hands his keys to the attendant and escorts his mother and me into the building.

"It's really unnecessary for me to be here. I'd be feeling perfectly fine if you'd have let me go home and change out of these wet clothes."

"Dad is bringing you dry clothes. Melanie will take good care of you."

We sign in at the desk and wait our turn to be called. Grace is registered before me. It's refreshing to be treated like everyone else in a hospital where they don't recognize my name or have a wing named after someone in my family.

We're escorted into the back together. There are a few private rooms, but most of the treatment areas are simply beds separated by sliding curtains. Grace and I are given beds in adjoining cubbies. Brady follows his mother into her little cube.

"Hi there. I'm Melanie, your nurse." A young, petite woman with dark brown hair and eyes to match walks into my little space with an armful of fabric. "We need to get you into something more comfortable." She chuckles to herself. "You know what I mean." She sets the pile onto the bed. "Here's a gown and some socks. Once you get into the bed, I'll bring a warm blanket." Melanie looks me up and down. "Why don't you hang your clothes over this chair here so they can dry. If you have a visitor, we'll bring in another chair."

"I won't be having any visitors."

She smiles again. "Okay. Well, please let me know

if you need any help."

She moves from my cubical to Grace's. Melanie was friendly with me, but she's downright chatty with Grace. I can hear their interactions clearly through the thin curtain that separates us. I begin to undress as instructed. It feels like the leathers weigh about fifty pounds, and maybe they do since the lining absorbed quite a bit of water.

"Kate called me and told me you were on your way. You poor thing. I'm just so glad you and Ms. Prescott are okay." I freeze in place with one arm out of my jacket. Does everyone here know everyone else, and are they always so nice? "Brady, please step outside so I can help your mom change into a gown."

I hear the swoosh of the curtain rail as Brady closes the curtain behind him. My cheeks feel warm when I think about him standing just outside. At least part of me is warm.

What do I look like in Brady's eyes? I can only imagine the state of my hair right now. I unzip my right jacket pocket and reach inside. The metal disk feels so cold against my skin. No matter. I wrap my fingers around the small compact and pull it out of my pocket.

The square compact looks just like it always does. I run my finger over the thin lines that run perpendicular to the edge. I hold my breath and open the compact.

I sigh in comfort at my unblemished reflection. The relief is by no means due to my appearance and my hair, which is plastered to the side of my head. No, my relief is because the mirror remains intact after my encounter with the pavement. Somehow my most treasured possession escaped this incident without a blemish.

The same cannot be said for me. A light purple haze seems to be growing down the outside of my thigh. My leg is sore, but it really doesn't feel as bad as it could considering what I went through. My biggest issue right now is the cold. I'm freezing. I bite my lip to keep my teeth from chattering as I continue to undress. My bra and panties are soaked through, so I remove them as well before slipping into the worn cotton hospital gown, and then I climb onto the bed.

"Ms. Prescott?" Melanie calls from the direction of Grace's cubby. "Are you ready for a blanket?"

"Yes, please."

Melanie slides open the curtain within seconds. My gaze locks with Brady who stands across the small hallway near the desk. He nods his head and walks out of sight. Melanie shakes out two warm blankets and lays them over me.

"You must be somebody special," she whispers with a curious smile.

"What do you mean?"

"Doctor Nevis just got a phone call from our state senator asking that we take really good care of you."

My face flushes bright red now. I know exactly why the hospital got a phone call about me, but I don't know how the channels could have moved so quickly.

Chapter Three

Brady

I may never get Vivienne's scent out of my car. The honeysuckle invades my senses as soon as I slide behind the wheel.

Why do I have to be the person Mom tasked with this errand? Not that I mind seeing Vivienne again, but there are many people who could bring her dinner tonight. It doesn't have to be me.

Mom made it sound like no other option made sense. Sure, I do own the best restaurant in town, and it is only a couple blocks from the Davidson Inn where Vivienne's staying tonight, but I still feel like there's more to this visit for Mom than simple food delivery. I'd accuse Mom of match-making except that Vivienne is leaving town tomorrow, so there's nowhere for this to go.

Lari, the owner of the inn, answers the door with her usual smile. She's a petite woman with short, sandy brown hair and a happy smile. She moved to Davidson and bought the inn from her uncle when he retired. Lari's children had gone off to college, and she felt she didn't have anyone left to take care of. Now she takes care of her guests and has the reputation of doing a phenomenal job.

"Good to see you, Brady. Your mother said you'd be by with dinner for that sweet girl I've got tucked in upstairs. She's in the first room on the right at the top of the stairs. I was just about to head up to bring her this extra quilt. Would you mind taking it to her?"

"Of course not."

I take the quilt from Lari and head upstairs to Vivienne's room. I'm struck with the intimacy of this moment. Walking upstairs to the bedroom of a beautiful woman. *Whom I know nothing about except that she is injured, rides a motorcycle, and doesn't live anywhere near here.* The intimate musings vanish.

Vivienne answers my knock after only a few long seconds wearing yoga pants and a purple t-shirt. Her honeysuckle scent wafts out to greet me.

"Hi, Brady. Won't you come in?"

"I brought you some dinner. Do you like braised pork?"

"That sounds amazing. Thank you. You can just

leave the bag there on the desk."

She motions to the antique wooden desk placed next to the door. I carefully set the bag down and hand Vivienne the blanket. "Lari asked me to bring this up to you."

"Thanks for that as well."

We stand together in the middle of her room. I take my first good look at it. The queen-sized, four-poster bed takes up the most room. It's covered with a soft-looking light blue comforter that matches the floral wallpaper. A large dresser and matching mirror take up the far wall. There's a set of antique chairs near a window across from the bed. It's very bed-and-breakfast-y, but the busy floral wallpaper is too much for me.

"I've never been inside this inn before."

"What do you think?"

"It could lose the floral wallpaper, but I love the woodwork and the furniture. I've often heard that Lari is a great hostess."

"She is. Lari's been very thoughtful." Vivienne smiles. "What do you have on your walls at home?"

A sigh escapes. "It's pretty much a bachelor pad. I have a large television and a leather couch. Do I really need anything else?"

Vivienne shrugs, and her smile grows. "I guess not. Do you live nearby?"

"Yeah, only a few blocks from here where the houses are much smaller than this one. I do have some nice crown molding and great transom windows."

"Do you live there alone?"

"I do."

I eye Vivienne a little closer. Is she just making conversation, or is this her way of finding out if I'm married. Maybe I wouldn't read anything into this conversation if our touch this morning hadn't felt like a spark that moved up my arm. She's the first woman in more than a year that I've noticed, and she doesn't even live here. I can't go down this path right now. I have to change the subject.

"How are you feeling? Any better?"

"The pain medication they gave me in the hospital is wearing off, but it honestly isn't as bad as I thought it would be."

"That's good news." I rack my brain for something to say to Vivienne to make polite conversation and learn more about her. If I can't think of anything to say, then I'll have to leave, and I'll never see her again.

"I really want to thank you for all your help today. I was so surprised after my slide, I might very well still be lying in the middle of the street if it weren't for you."

My eyes are drawn to Vivienne's lips and the small smile on them.

"I don't think that's true. You were really lucky to take a slide like that and come out of it as nicely as you did."

"Still, you and your mother, and everyone in

Davidson, have been so kind. I'm not used to people being so nice to me without wanting anything in return."

"That's ridiculous. What do you mean?"

"I think that's what most relationships are about. It's all very civilized, but people want things from each other. That's how the world works."

"That isn't how Davidson works. Here we do nice things for each other out of the kindness of our hearts." She blushes slightly, her cheeks turning a light pink. I'm sure the coloring was a reaction to my argument, but if it makes her cheeks take on such a rosy glow, then I'm happy to argue with her a lot more.

"I think you're right. I truly appreciate all you've done for me, Brady. Please pass on my thanks to your mom and sister as well."

"I will. May I plate your food for you?"

"That won't be necessary. I can do it."

"Well, then I guess I'll be going."

I turn and force myself to walk to the door. Vivienne follows me and places her hand on the doorknob.

"Goodnight, Brady. I hope you have a good evening at your restaurant."

I look down at her and take in the sight of her wide, caramel eyes one last time. Her pink lips part slightly. For several long seconds neither of us move. My gaze moves from her lips to her chest. I watch as her breasts rise and fall with each shaky breath. Her hand falls to her side. The air between us is full of electrical charge. My gaze again meets Vivienne's. She feels this moment, too.

The question is, what should I do about it?

I could kiss her, which is exactly what my body wants me to do. Maybe everyone needs the memories of a romantic encounter with a beautiful stranger. No strings attached. It's a quality many men look for in a woman.

Of course, I've never been like most men in that department. The reality for me is that if anything happened between us, I'd pine for Vivienne after she left town. My heart would be broken again, which is exactly what I'm supposed to be protecting myself from.

I take a deep breath, stand as tall as I can, and clasp the doorknob.

"I have to get back to work. I don't have time for this."

I take one last look at her big brown eyes and leave the room. I'm not sure exactly what I thought I was supposed to do in there, but my brain is clearly disappointed in me. If it isn't enough that I didn't kiss the woman, I was rude and ran away. Not my best moment, but it doesn't matter because I will never see her again.

Chapter Four

Viv

I squint my eyes to try to see into the parking lot. It's useless. The pounding rain thrashes against the large, plate-glass window of the diner. I sigh to myself. This nasty weather is forecasted to continue all day. It looks like I'll be staying at the Davidson Inn another night. I don't know if I can summon the courage to get back on my bike in the first place, but I'm especially not going to ride it in this weather.

Spending another night here will delay my trip home. Is that good or bad? It's good because I'm not ready to face the decisions that await me there. It's bad because I need to stop avoiding my future and what Grandmother has planned for me. That's partly what this whole trip has been about—my future, not the avoiding Grandmother part.

If I wasn't so stubborn, I would just ditch the Harley and buy a car. I won't do it. I had to fight Grandmother tooth and nail to leave town on that motorcycle. I certainly don't want her to have any reason to think my jaunt was a failure.

Maybe my journey of self-discovery wasn't a total failure, but it certainly wasn't what I thought it would be. I thought I would be painting every morning and driving from one beautiful destination to another. I pictured myself making connections with people I met along the way. That isn't what my trip has been like at all.

I did meet some nice people but never anyone I saw myself staying in touch with. Of course, I'm the one to blame for my lack of encounters since I didn't put myself out there enough to get to know anyone.

There was no painting either. I saw amazing sunrises over the ocean and sunsets over the mountains, and I never once had the urge to bring my paintbrush to the canvas. That's my biggest regret from this trip, although there's nothing I can do about it.

Am I really on this adventure in an effort to find myself, or am I merely trying to postpone the inevitable? I've been gone for almost six months, and I still don't know the answer to that question.

"More coffee, sweetie?" I nod, and the plump waitress pours more into my cup. "Anything else, hon?"

"How about a piece of that apple pie?"

Defeat.

I've been sitting on this stool for the last two hours staring at the glass case of desserts. After the breakfast I ate of biscuits and gravy—something newly discovered on this journey—the last thing I need is dessert. But, a person can only be so strong. There's fruit in the pie. Does that count? That can be healthy and must at least be better for me than the chocolate layer cake or thick custard I could have chosen.

The waitress plops a large piece of pie in front of me. Definitely not healthy, but I dive in anyway.

Boisterous laughter causes me and several other nearby patrons to look up from our food. Kate Richardson walks into the diner with the other woman who helped out after the incident yesterday. They laugh together as they shake off the rain and then walk over to me. I spin around on my stool to greet them in time for Kate to lean in for a hello hug.

"So nice to see you again, Viv," Kate says sweetly. "This is Meg McMann. She was with us on the street yesterday, but with everything going on, I'm sure you don't remember."

"I do. Thank you for your assistance yesterday."

Meg smiles, but the gesture doesn't go to her eyes. Something is clearly on her mind. The two ladies take the empty stools next to me at the counter.

"Hi there, Melinda," Kate says cheerily to the waitress. "We'll take two specials."

Grandmother would declare Kate's red hair and freckles to be *unfortunate genetics*. On this woman, however, the features aren't unfortunate at all. She's gorgeous, and despite the fact that her hair is pretty much soaked, she has a happy glow about her.

"How're you feeling, Kate?"

Her hand moves to her stomach. "Good. I think the morning sickness phase is over."

Kate's pregnant? How did I miss this yesterday?

"Glad to hear it. I'll have your chicken pot pies in just a sec."

"Congratulations on your pregnancy. I had no idea."

Her smile grows. "Things were a little hectic yesterday."

"When are you due? Do you know if the baby is a girl or a boy?"

"My due date is May thirtieth. We asked our doctor to write the sex of our baby on a paper and seal it inside an envelope. Hunter and I plan to open it on Christmas Eve."

"That's so sweet."

Kate's smile grows. "Did you have the chicken pot pie?"

"No, I had the biscuits and gravy."

"A solid choice," Meg comments. She has long, blond hair and bright blue eyes. Her accent sounds out of place in this little Virginia town, almost literally. Brooklyn maybe? Somewhere up north, and something I haven't heard much at all on this adventure.

Melinda places two large platters in front of the ladies. Each has an individual pan of chicken pot pie covered in a golden, flaky crust similar to what covered my apple pie. Meg digs in with her fork. Steam is released, and I can now see the chunks of chicken, carrot, and potato inside. Maybe I should have tried chicken pot pie. Of course, if the rain doesn't stop, I might still be sitting here at dinner time.

"Wow. Looking at that makes me sorry I didn't order it. How do you stay thin, living in this town?"

Kate laughs. "It's a challenge, I assure you. If this food wasn't good enough, Meg here's a chef. She's amazing."

Meg scoffs. "I don't know about that, and it won't matter what kind of a chef I am if we can't find someone to replace Rhonda. We're busier than we've ever been." Her eyes meet mine for a thoughtful second. "You don't have any fine dining service experience by any chance?"

"No. Sorry. I have lots of experience eating in restaurants, but I've never had a job as a waitress." Or any job for that matter. They don't need to know that part.

"Do you know wine?"

"Sure."

"What's your favorite?"

Is this a test? I feel like we're doing more than making conversation.

"Well, I have a few favorites. I generally prefer French wine, especially Châteauneuf-du-Pape. I know many people prefer wine from Burgundy or Bordeaux, but I have always loved the richness of the Châteauneuf-du-Pape region. As far as California, I think Opus One is quite lovely."

"Well, you certainly know your *expensive* wine."

Meg smiles now and then studies me for a few seconds. I can't blame her. Women dressed in leather riding pants don't typically know wine and use words like *lovely*.

"I didn't get to talk with you much yesterday. Do you live in Virginia?"

"No, I'm just passing through." I heard that in a movie once, and it fits my situation. "I planned on leaving town today, but the weather still isn't cooperating."

"Is your leg well enough to ride?"

I stick out my leg and bend it at the knee a couple times as if to check it out. "I'm a little sore, but it's fine." Truthfully, I'm a lot sore, but not enough that I couldn't ride out of here if the weather was better.

"I have an idea. Just hear me out before you decline my offer." Meg takes a deep breath and releases it. "I'm the chef at Mayfair. Brady and I own the restaurant."

"Then you made that incredible braised pork I had for dinner last night."

Meg smiles. "I'm glad you liked it, but how did you get it?"

"Grace asked Brady to bring me something to eat. She didn't have to take care of me, but she did. She's such a lovely woman."

"Very true. Mom likes to take care of everyone."

"You're very lucky."

"Okay. Back to my offer," Meg chimes in. Right. The conversation had drifted. I'd forgotten Meg was about to propose something. She takes a deep breath and continues. "Rhonda, our best server, had to have an emergency appendectomy yesterday. With it being the holidays and all, we have no one to replace her. Kennedy was able to help out last night after her day shift here at Minnie's, but she can't continue with that schedule. Besides the fact that Kennedy can't work so many hours, she's working the dinner shift here tonight and isn't available to work at Mayfair. We're in a seriously tight spot. Is there any chance you'd consider taking Rhonda's place tonight? Maybe by tomorrow we can find someone to fill in for her until she returns."

Um. A job?

"As I have already mentioned, I have no experience."

"Being a waitress is the easy part. You take their order and bring them their food. You speak well, and you know wine. Knowing the wine is the most difficult part for most people. You can learn the rest."

"You don't even know me."

She and Kate share a look. "I've seen enough to know I like you. Besides, if you're stuck in Davidson anyway, you might as well make the most of it and earn some money, right?"

"I don't know."

I look out the window. It's still raining cats and dogs. I have nothing else to do. Should I give it a try? Should I be worried about how quickly this came about? As a single woman traveling around, I've been extra cautious. What if all the kindness shown by these people is really some intricate plot against me? Grace and Brady could have kidnapped me and held me for ransom yesterday, but they didn't.

The thought is completely ridiculous. I sound as paranoid as Grandmother. These people are genuine. Grace, Brady, Kate, and now Meg have been nothing but helpful to me since I've been here in Davidson. Somehow I just know they're okay.

Meg isn't offering another volunteer effort that someone has cooked up to look good in society. This is an actual job that pays an actual, real salary. Grandmother would utterly flip out if she learned I was working. I've always wondered what it would be like to earn a paycheck. This may be the only chance I ever have to find out. A giddiness begins to build inside me at the thought. What would it be like to give Grandmother the news that a Prescott is working as a waitress? Whether it's a fancy restaurant or this diner, the news might give Grandmother a heart attack.

"I'll do it," I say. Meg squeals. "Just for tonight though. I do have to get back on the road tomorrow."

As much as I dread the thought of getting back to my reality, I can't put it off any longer.

"I'll take it. You've made my day." No longer down, Meg takes a huge bite of her lunch. "Brady'll be so relieved."

Considering how quickly he ran away from me last night, I'm not so sure about that.

Chapter Five

Brady

"I've solved our problem."

Meg stands before me with her hands on her hips and a huge grin on her face. She closes the door to the office behind her.

"You've found someone to replace Rhonda?"

"Yes, for tonight, anyway. Viv is still stuck in town because of the rain. She's agreed to work tonight."

My body has an immediate reaction. My blood seems to have travelled straight to my groin. I've been thinking all day that she'd left town this morning, and she's been here all along. I try to keep all of this on the inside. I'm not sure how successful I am with that effort.

"Vivienne? What kind of experience does she have?"

"She can handle it. Don't worry."

That doesn't answer my question.

"Wait a minute. We just met this woman yesterday, we know basically nothing about her, and you offered her a job?"

Meg frowns and cocks her head to the side to convey her disappointment.

"Yes. It'll be great. You'll see."

"Is she here now?"

"Just outside. Come and say hello."

With a heavy sigh, I heave myself up from my desk and walk into the dining room. Vivienne's there, alright. She wears her black leather jacket and leather pants with a big scrape down the left leg where she slid her bike yesterday.

I guess some guys are into the leather look. I'm not one of them. I prefer the softer version of Vivienne I saw at the inn last night.

She holds out her hand.

"Very nice to see you again, Brady."

Two quick pumps of my hand is all I give her for a handshake before I force myself let go.

How I feel when I touch this woman aside, what the hell was Meg thinking? Mayfair has an image to uphold. Leather-clad biker chicks are not the type of person we hire. Our customers have come to expect a classy experience when they eat at our restaurant. Vivienne isn't right for this position.

"Do you have any experience?" The words come out a little harsher than I intended. I open my mouth to take them back, but what's the point? The question needs to be asked.

"No, but I'm confident I can handle it."

"Waiting tables is one of the hardest jobs there is. What makes you think you can *handle it*?"

Meg cuts me a look of disapproval. I don't blame her. It isn't like me to be rude, but I can't protect myself from falling for Vivienne if she's here under my nose all night.

"I'll do my best. I can promise you that." Her mocha eyes brighten with confidence.

"You'll have to wear a uniform."

"Of course. Meg has gone over the required attire." She looks down at her own outfit. "You have no need to worry. I only wear the leathers when I'm riding. I dressed in these because I thought I'd be riding today. Given that the rain is still with us, I've decided to postpone my departure."

What kind of biker chick uses words like *attire* and *postpone my departure*?

"Brady, don't be such a snob. Viv's going to be great. Come with me, Viv. We can call Lari to get your room reserved, and then I'll show you around the kitchen."

"Do not be concerned, Brady. I can do this."

Meg smiles. How can she be so confident Vivienne will work out? But, it's only one night and having someone take Rhonda's place is better than having no one. In theory.

"Vivienne can help us with waiting on our guests, but I don't think it's a good idea if she handles the checks."

Wrong thing to say.

I watch as the cheeks of both women flush with anger.

"That is so insulting." Meg's the first one to let her feelings be known.

"No, Brady's right. It takes time to build trust—for some longer than others. Brady has only known me for a short time."

Maybe this woman does have some sense after all.

"You're right, but that isn't all I was thinking about. The credit card system can be frustrating. I'd rather you spend what little time we have this afternoon learning about the menu and how we take care of our guests." Viv's eyes soften. "And you will still have to fill out your employment forms. Just because you'll only be working here for one night doesn't mean we aren't going to be legal about this."

Vivienne breaks eye contact and looks away—not a good sign. She sighs, arches her back, and looks at me again. "That's fine. I will complete whatever paperwork you would like. However, I do have one condition."

"What's that?"

"If anyone ever calls to confirm my employment here at Mayfair, I would like you to tell them you have no record of my working here." My mouth opens. "I mean, you can confirm my employment with any official government agency, but no one else can know."

"Are you hiding from someone? Is there some situation we need to be aware of?"

She forces a smile. "Oh, no. Nothing like that. I simply do not wish for others to know I was employed here. That is all. I am sure no one will call. It is only a precaution."

There's definitely something here, but the request isn't completely unreasonable.

"Thanks for helping us out."

Vivienne manages a small smile before she turns, and follows Meg toward the kitchen.

This is going to be a disaster.

What kind of woman doesn't have a job and is just *passing through*? This thought conjures up images of a hippie back in the sixties. While Vivienne dresses like she's in a biker gang, she seems to be traveling alone, and besides, she sure doesn't speak like she lives that kind of life. Her voice is soft and measured with no detectable accent. It's very pleasant and precise, as if each word is carefully vetted prior to leaving her mouth. She'll do very well with speaking to the Mayfair guests.

Meg and Vivienne had a mini-training session

earlier this afternoon. She seems to have the hang of what to say while waiting on our guests. Hopefully, Vivienne will be able to perform the tasks when our guests are here, and the pressure is on. I'll handle all of her credit card and money transactions. Despite what I said about the credit card machine, we know very little about her, and I don't want her handling money or our customers' credit cards.

Still, I can't trust her to spend time with our customers without knowing more about her. When we hired Katherine, Leo, and Manny, there was time to get to know them. We even did a criminal background check.

Maybe there isn't time for an official background review, but I'm not powerless. Doubtful that much of anything is going to come up in an Internet search on a woman who's *just passing through*, I type Vivienne's name into the search engine anyway and hit enter.

Wow.

Links and images fill my screen. The photos are definitely of Vivienne, but her look is much different than the Vivienne I saw earlier this afternoon. In most of the photos, she's wearing fancy, full-length gowns, and she's on the arm of some handsome dude in a tuxedo. The caption of the first photo reads *Prescott Family Donates $2.4 Million to Children's Charity*. An article from the *Boston Globe* dated April 19th of this year accompanies the photo.

> *The 27th Annual Spring for Sunshine Gala raised a record-breaking $1.2 million this year. In what has become a tradition, the Prescott family has again generously matched the donations, kicking in an additional $1.2 million for the charity. Mrs. Eleanor Prescott chaired the event with her granddaughter, Vivienne Prescott, seen in photo with long-time family friend, Henry Withers.*

The article goes on to list past donations and the Prescott's love for children and charity. Two—no three things—stick in my mind. Vivienne is a knockout in that dress. I can hardly believe the woman in this photo wearing who knows what kind of designer dress and chunks of diamonds around her neck is the same person who was just standing here wearing leather biker pants.

And who is this Henry guy? Someone who's loaded obviously. I don't know tuxes, but I do know that rentals don't fit as perfectly as this one does. Why does the sneery smile of Vivienne's *family friend* bother me?

Could Vivienne really be this loaded? Seriously? I gave a five hundred-dollar donation to the American Cancer Society last month. I thought that was a hefty sum. Millions? Well, that's a whole new concept.

My phone alarm announces that it's time for our daily staff meeting. How can it possibly be four thirty already? With a heavy sigh, I push away from my desk and head to the kitchen. We get together every afternoon at this time to go over specials and any other information we need to discuss with the staff.

We're a small group. We have five servers, and two of them are out of town for Christmas. That's what makes the timing of Rhonda's surgery even worse. If it was not the holiday season, we could just call someone in from their day off. Unfortunately, Rhonda's appendix couldn't have decided to go haywire at a worse time. Truthfully, I'm just glad she's going to be okay.

This is going to be fine.

Our servers, Katherine and Manny, are here and ready to go, along with Meg and her assistant, Leo.

"Rhonda's out of surgery," Katherine announces happily. "Her husband told me it was pretty bad. Her appendix almost ruptured. It was really serious. If she'd waited much longer to get to the hospital, she could have died."

"Not to be insensitive or anything"—Manny sighs heavily and looks around at the rest of us—"But, what are we going to do to replace Rhonda while she's recuperating? The doctor said it could take a month or more for her to be back to work, and we're slammed right now."

"We'll just have to take the situation day by day. For tonight, we have someone to help us."

"Really? Who?"

Right on cue, Vivienne walks into the kitchen—at

least I think it's Vivienne. She's had a complete transformation. This version matches the one from the newspaper photo. If I hadn't just seen the society photos, I might not believe her to be the same person.

The black uniform pants and tuxedo shirt fit her curves nicely, although not as nicely as the formal gowns in those photos. She wears very little makeup, but she still seems put together. Maybe it's the fact that her hair is pulled back in a tight bun, or maybe it's the tuxedo that does that—of course it's nothing like the fancy duds her friend, Henry, was wearing in that photo. It's as if I'm meeting a whole new woman. I would never guess this is the same motorcycle mama from a few hours ago. She could just as soon be a ballerina.

Vivienne smiles and moves her gaze over the kitchen and the people in it. Our eyes meet and lock. Her smile grows.

Right. Time for her introduction.

I swallow and clear my throat.

"Everyone, this is Vivienne. She's going to be helping us out for tonight. Vivienne, this is Leo. He's Meg's assistant here in the kitchen." Vivienne shakes Leo's hand. "This is Katherine and Manny. They'll be serving with you." They both shake her hand in turn.

"It's very nice to meet you. Please call me Viv, and I'm sorry to hear about your friend, Rhonda."

Katherine returns her smile. "Let us know if there's anything we can do to help you tonight. It can get pretty slammed at times."

"Thank you for your kind offer. I appreciate it very much."

There it is again. That soft voice that fits her wealthy status much better than the biker chick I met yesterday. Is this a twin? Maybe I'm being punked? I make eye contact with Meg. She smiles an *I-told-you-so* smile and then turns to the group, launching into her descriptions of tonight's specials.

Chapter Six

Viv

Working is harder than it looks, but I'm loving every minute of it. Well, almost every minute. There was an incident earlier in the evening when the water pitcher slipped from my hand and broke. Manny helped me clean it up, and it was as if the incident never happened.

Mostly, being a waitress here has a lot to do with memory. I don't mean remembering the person's order when they tell me. I make sure to write their orders down. I'm not willing to risk forgetting, and I don't care to show off my waitressing skills by remembering details about what entree someone wants for dinner. I'm only here one night, and I want this night to be a success.

The trick is remembering many details at once. I have to remember the status of the meal at each table and keep the timing of their dining experience moving at the right flow. Fine dining isn't about quick service, but you can't leave a guest waiting forever for a drink refill either. You have to be on top of everything. I know this from my own experience as a customer, and I want to do my best to give the people I wait on exceptional service. This may be my only chance at ever having a real job. I want it to be the best night possible.

Five tables have been assigned to me to look after this evening, and they are the tables located closest to the kitchen. Brady thought that would be the easiest for me since that means less of a distance to carry plates of food. I think he's hedging his bets that it's less likely for something to go wrong. That's okay with me. He's probably right.

I can see why Brady's so protective of Mayfair. He and Meg have created an impressive place to dine. The ambiance is characteristic of fine dining but with a charm lacking in most restaurants of this caliber. I've eaten at too many fancy places to count, and they're mostly the same. Sure, the food is impeccable, and the service is good, but most of them are trying too hard. Sometimes their food is so fancy that it's no longer delicious. The atmosphere is so elegant that it is no longer comfortable. Mayfair is special all around, and the little bits of Meg's cooking I tasted last night and earlier this afternoon were amazing. She could easily be a chef in New York or Paris or anywhere else she wishes. Yet, she chooses to be here in this minute Virginia town, which is somehow special on its own.

Now, it's just after six o'clock, and almost every table in the place is full. Most of the tables seat two or four guests. There is one in Katherine's section that seats ten and is filled with extended family and two children under five years old. She has her hands full. I'm relieved that Brady assigned me to the back of the restaurant where no one can watch me. Well, except for Brady. He pretty much hasn't taken his eyes off of me this evening, but I suppose that's to be expected.

Brady escorts a couple to the back of the Mayfair dining room and seats them at my last empty table. The man appears to be in his sixties. He's portly, with silver hair and blue-gray eyes. His wife is a little on the heavy side. She also has silver hair that she's pulled back into a bun. They look like they're dressed up for a nice night out. Brady's gaze locks with mine. We approach the table together.

Deep breath.

"This is your server, Vivienne. Vivienne, this is Police Chief Tisdale and his wife, Maybelle. They're having dinner with us tonight to celebrate their anniversary."

"How very wonderful to meet you both." Brady nods to Chief Tisdale and walks back to his spot at the front of the restaurant. I turn to the couple. There's no question they're still in love with each other. What a funny thought. I've just barely met them, and yet, I can tell. It's in the soft way they look at each other. "May I ask how many years you've been married?"

"Forty-two years," Mrs. Tisdale says with a smile.

"How wonderful. I'm happy to be here with you tonight to help you celebrate. Do you eat here at Mayfair often?"

"Oh, no," Chief Tisdale says with a chuckle. An image of Santa Claus pops into my head. While he does have the belly that jiggles like jelly, the chief has no facial hair. It must just be the time of year that encouraged that thought. Christmas is only three days away. "If we go out at all, we usually go to Minnie's. We did come here once over the summer not long after Brady opened this place, but we haven't been back since. We're saving our visits to Mayfair for celebrations."

"We will definitely celebrate tonight."

"What's your last name, Vivienne?" Mrs. Tisdale smiles at me and gives her head a little tilt. "It's just that I know most everyone in this town, and I don't think I've ever seen you before."

"Prescott. I'm Vivienne Prescott." I spare Mrs. Tisdale the woes of traveling by motorcycle. "I'm new to Davidson and only visiting for a short time."

"Well, Mel and I are so happy to have you with us tonight."

Her beaming smile and kind eyes are so welcoming. Everyone in this town is so friendly.

"Thank you. I will ensure that the two of you have a fantastic anniversary. May I bring you a cocktail while you peruse the menu? Or, maybe some champagne?"

Mrs. Tisdale's eyes twinkle at the mention of champagne. The chief catches on right away—as he should after being married to his love for forty-two years.

"Champagne it is. We aren't fussy. Please bring us something inexpensive. I'm sure Brady doesn't stock junk in his fancy restaurant. I don't care for champagne too much in the first place, so there's no point in paying a fortune for a bottle. Am I right?"

Not according to Grandmother. I've had cheap sparkling wine a couple times. I don't want to sound like a snob, but there is a huge difference. I don't lecture my guests on the pros and cons of good champagne. Instead, I return Mrs. Tisdale's shy smile with a confident one, which isn't forced, but isn't necessarily the result of the chief's comment. I can't let these sweet people drink the cheapest champagne available on their special night.

"Let me see what I can find for you."

I head into the kitchen to see what vintages are kept in the chiller. I spent a little time in here with Meg this afternoon to review where the wine and champagne are kept, but we mostly focused on the wine. Now, I spend a few moments studying the choices. There are three inexpensive champagne choices. I haven't ever tried any of them.

The vintage makes a difference. The inexpensive options Brady has in stock are not poor quality by any means, but they aren't truly champagne. They're from California. So while they may be delicious, they aren't from the Champagne region of France. I can't help but be a snob about this. That's what happens when a person spends as much time in France as I have. Brady stocks only two French champagnes. I choose the bottle that will make the best impression.

This is the Tisdale's anniversary. I want to make it special for them. However, it's clear that they would not want to pay two hundred and fifty dollars for a bottle of champagne.

Dom it is.

I walk quickly back to their table with the champagne—real, actual champagne and not the imposter-California stuff. Geez, I sound as snotty as Grandmother does when discussing this subject.

"This is a bottle that Brady has been holding for a special occasion. He'd like to give it to you as a gift in honor of your special night."

"What is it?" Mrs. Tisdale asks curiously.

I turn the label so she can see the bottle. Her eyes widen. She gasps and then breaks out into a huge smile. I begin removing the foil to get to the cork.

"Everything okay here?" Brady. Of course.

"Everything is wonderful. I was just sharing the

news that you would like to treat the Tisdales to a bottle of champagne as a good wish for their anniversary."

Mr. And Mrs. Tisdale turn toward Brady. He slaps a nervous smile on his face to cover and looks at me. I give him a wink. He makes eye contact again with both Mr. And Mrs. Tisdale in turn and relaxes enough that hopefully neither can tell that Brady's not clear on what's happening here. I remove the rest of the foil.

"Would you care to do the honors, Brady?"

"You go right ahead. I think this is your party."

Brady can't really think that I would give this expensive bottle of champagne away without paying for it, can he? Maybe. He seems extremely uncomfortable. He stands in the same spot and watches me as I pour Mrs. Tisdale a glass and then Mr. Tisdale.

"Enjoy. I will be back very soon to check on you."

Brady nods to the couple and follows me as I walk towards the kitchen, grabbing an empty bread basket from one of my other tables. He lays into me as soon as we round the corner and are fully in the kitchen.

"What the hell was that all about?"

Brady does nothing to disguise his anger. It practically spills out of him. If his tone didn't give it away, the brightness of his face certainly would have. Brady has a light complexion with a few freckles. When he's angry, his face turns a deep red. Thank goodness he held it together until we were away from the restaurant guests.

Meg and Leo both look up from their work. I make brief eye contact with Meg before looking again at Brady. I take a step closer to Brady and continue our conversation in a hushed tone so that hopefully no one else will hear our discussion.

"Do I have to get your permission for everything I buy here? Is that part of my job duties?"

"You didn't buy that champagne. You said it was on the house."

"I said that so the Tisdales would accept it. If they knew it was a gift from me, they wouldn't drink it."

"Why would you buy a bottle of Dom Pérignon for people you don't even know?"

"I wanted to make their anniversary even more special. Mrs. Tisdale said she didn't like champagne. I just thought she should try the real thing before she decided."

"Why would you give me the credit?"

"Why not? I don't need credit for anything. I only meant it as a nice gesture. It was a bit whimsical, but it isn't a big deal."

"It's a very big deal. That's only the second bottle of Dom that we've sold since Mayfair opened."

"Well, that's a shame."

The words fly out in a snotty tone that I wish I could take back. My flared temper isn't just from this one encounter with Brady. I've had plenty of experience with people back home questioning my motives. I despise it when people expect the worst of me or think I have some hidden agenda. I can't do something nice for someone just to be nice? I thought this kind of distrust was only found in the snobby society back home. Apparently, people question your motives whether they know you or not. I move my hands to my hips and stand as tall as I can to hold my ground against Brady. He still has several inches on me.

Brady runs his hand through his hair and sighs heavily.

"Did you really mean to buy that champagne all along, or are you just saying this to get yourself out of hot water?"

"Are you always this distrustful of people, or is it only me?"

"It wasn't right for me to jump on your case without asking first. I couldn't understand why you'd buy something so expensive for people you don't even know. That bottle costs more than you're going to make tonight. Do you realize that?"

I raise an eyebrow. "Is this how you treat all of your employees?"

"You've given me no reason to distrust you. I'm sorry for letting this get out of control. I'm not going to get into it, but let's just say I've not had the best of luck when it comes to trusting people. I inevitably get burned."

The redness has left Brady's cheeks. His

expression has softened. I can't stay mad at him. If he has had trust issues in the past, then I need to let him off the hook. I'm only here for one night. Why hold a grudge?

"I accept your apology." The corners of his lips lift into a small smile. "You need to understand something about me, though. I abhor lying, and I would never lie to you or anyone else."

"Good to know, but *never* isn't long with you. You're leaving town tomorrow."

"Then can I get back to work? I have a lot to do."

Chapter Seven

Brady

Vivienne isn't easy to figure out. She's worldly but somehow not, at the same time. She just sold a bottle of one of my most expensive French wines to a couple from Charlottesville and talked expertly about visiting the vineyard in Châteauneuf-du-Pape. Why does a person with that kind of money ride around on a motorcycle giving away fancy champagne on a whim?

Why is an heiress here in Davidson and working in my restaurant? Is this her idea of charity work? Bringing fancy wine and champagne to the little people?

She did pay for that bottle of champagne within a

few minutes of our conversation. I sold it to her at cost, but she'll be lucky to make that much money in tips tonight. Of course, if she keeps selling the expensive wine, she won't have any issues recovering the money in tips. Not that any of that matters to someone with millions or billions of dollars in the bank.

Vivienne seems unsure and occasionally even nervous when she approaches a table for the first time. In no time, she seems to have charmed her guests until it looks more like they're all old friends.

My own mother acts like Vivienne is her long-lost relative. It's just like her to take in every stray she can find and feed them, but Mom seems even more attached to Vivienne than usual. Mom called thirty minutes ago to make sure I'm not over-working Vivienne after her accident. I tried to explain that I had nothing to do with hiring her. That didn't work. Mom made it clear to me that if Vivienne overdoes it tonight, the blame is solely on my shoulders.

How did Vivienne work that magic with Mom and with Meg, too, for that matter? It isn't like Meg to trust strangers at all. So Meg liked Vivienne when she first met her. That doesn't mean she needed to hire her to work here. And only for one night. Granted, we seriously needed someone to help out, but we'll be in the same boat tomorrow.

Meg put a considerable amount of effort into training Vivienne for one night of work. Was the effort worth it? Honestly, despite the champagne dust-up and the fact that she has no experience, Vivienne is actually doing a pretty good job. Given what I read about her online, she likely has a lot of experience eating in restaurants much fancier than Mayfair. Maybe I can convince Vivienne to stay a little longer. She's trained now and has a night of experience, so maybe she would consider staying a little longer. It'll probably require a lot of groveling after the way I treated her earlier, but I have to try. I can enlist Meg's help if I have to.

"That was quite a dinner, Brady." Chief Tisdale and Maybelle stand next to me near the front door. I was so lost in thought that I didn't even see them walk up. The chief pats his full belly.

"I hope we made your anniversary celebration special."

"You sure did. Thanks again for the champagne. That was awfully sweet of you. I didn't think I really cared much for champagne, but now I know I just like the good stuff." Mrs. Tisdale pauses and gives me a quick hug. "Mel might not thank you since my new taste for fine champagne will likely cost him in the future, but it was sure a nice touch for tonight."

How can I take credit for Vivienne's kind gesture? I can't tell the Tisdales the truth now, so I play along, and we share a chuckle—I sure hope mine isn't too forced.

"You are both very welcome. Forty-two years of marriage is worthy of a big celebration." The chief smiles and extends his hand for a shake.

"That Viv is such a lovely young woman," Maybelle adds. "I hope she'll be in town for a while."

"Me, too. Thanks for coming in tonight."

The chief takes his wife's hand and leads her out the door. My gaze meets Vivienne's from across the room. She smiles, and my chest warms. I push the feeling away, avert my eyes, and get back to work, which is what I should have been doing in the first place.

The phone rings, and I answer with my usual, "It's a lovely evening at Mayfair. How may I assist you?"

"May I speak with Vivienne please?"

The man's voice is gruff, but he uses a polite tone. My stomach instantly burns. It's Vivienne's first night working here, and she's getting a personal call already? Really?

"One moment please." I force my tone to remain polite despite the anger churning. Is it really because Vivienne got a personal call, or is it because the caller is male?

This is stupid. Of course my anger stems from the personal call bit. Why would I care who calls my very temporary employee?

I hit the hold button and walk to Vivienne's section. She looks up at me with a smile that morphs into confusion. I will my expression to regulate to something more manageable.

Vivienne pauses with a small stack of the

Tisdale's dirty dessert dishes in her hands. "Is something wrong?"

"You have a phone call. You can take it in my office."

Her face pales. "I have a phone call? They asked for me personally?"

"Yes."

"Did you tell them I work here?"

Right. The agreement we made this afternoon was that I would not verify Vivienne's employment with anyone unofficial, and a man calling at nine o'clock is hardly a government official on the clock. What did I even say? I was immediately concerned with the fact that a man was calling here to speak with Vivienne.

"Did you?"

"No. I just put the call on hold."

The relief that washes across her face is palpable. Who is she worried about? A reporter maybe? Would that be news in Boston, that a socialite has a job as a waitress?

"Please tell them no one by that name works here."

"I will. I'm sorry I didn't do that right away. I wasn't thinking."

"It's okay. No harm done."

I quietly walk back to the hostess stand where I spend much of my evenings. The little orange light blinks to show that the call remains on hold.

"Who are you holding for?"

"Vivienne? Is she working tonight?"

"Sorry, sir. No one by that name works here." I quickly disconnect the call before the man has a chance to ask any more questions and turn to see Vivienne watching me from across the room. What kind of secrets is this woman hiding?

❖❖❖

"You did well tonight. You've really never had a serving job before?"

Vivienne shakes her head. "It was fun."

Fun. That isn't a word normally used to describe this job. I mean there are worse jobs for sure, but this is still a job. Leo and Katherine wear their exhaustion on their faces. Vivienne is somehow smiling from ear to ear.

"Well, you certainly had a good night."

"Thank you so much, Viv, for helping us out tonight." Meg hugs Vivienne.

"No, thank you. This was a lot of fun."

There it is again—*fun*. Meg smiles. "I really wish you could stay longer. Not just to help us out, but it's been great getting to know you. Make sure you stay in touch. Okay?"

Vivienne nods and gives Meg another hug.

"Thanks to you all."

Vivienne makes eye contact with Meg and then me. She's wearing her leather jacket over her Mayfair uniform. The leather biker look seems at odds now with the woman who gifts expensive bottles of champagne to strangers. It's as if she's wearing her boyfriend's jacket, like it couldn't possibly be her own. I'm intrigued. What other crazy things does she do? Does she buy smart phones for the poor kids who can only afford the flip version?

Still. Something about her makes me want to know more. Maybe it's because she's different from anyone else I've ever met. Maybe I'm drawn to her spunk. Or more likely, I can't get the picture of Vivienne in that low-cut gown out of my head.

"Let me walk you to the inn."

"You don't have to. It's only a couple blocks."

"I'd like to anyway. Just let me grab my coat, and we can go out through the back."

Vivienne follows me down the short hallway to the office. I grab my coat and my keys. I could offer to drive her, but walking seems like a better idea. She's leaving tomorrow. Nothing is going to happen between us, so maybe it's okay if I allow myself a quick thought or two about *what if*? She's a beautiful woman, and I've been in a self-imposed drought for more than a year. This is just a walk. Nothing more.

The cool night air is refreshing after the heat of the kitchen. I take a deep breath and let the crisp air fill my lungs. Vivienne zips up her coat and folds her arms in front of her.

"You really don't have to walk me back, you know. I can handle it."

"I'm sure you could, but you never know what

the mean streets of Davidson could throw at you." My comment gets the desired effect. She smiles, revealing perfect white teeth.

We come around the corner out of the back alley and make a left turn onto Cherry Street. "The rain has finally stopped, but the high for tomorrow is forecasted to be in the forties. It doesn't bother you to ride in the cold."

"I'm not a big fan, truthfully. That's why I need to get home before it turns even colder."

"You're going to ride all the way to Boston in this weather?"

I only know that's where she lives because of the address she wrote on her tax form. Meg thought I was silly for making Vivienne fill out employment forms for only one night of work, but without that, I would know even less about her.

Vivienne sighs. "Yes, that's the plan. I have been putting the trip off for too long. Now, I only have two days to get there."

"Who called you earlier?" I've been avoiding asking the question, but I have to. I can't let this be something I wonder about for the rest of my life.

Vivienne's eyes widen, but just slightly before she shrugs her shoulders. "I'm not sure, but no one is supposed to know where I am. The person I'm closest with has my cell number. If it was an emergency, that's the number they would have called.

Is the person she's closest with a man or a

woman? I guess that's a question that will be a mystery for the rest of my life because I've intruded on Vivienne's life enough.

We walk in silence and make the left turn onto Elm. There's less than a block left. I can see the inn up ahead. My time with Vivienne is almost over. I don't miss the irony that I didn't trust her to work at Mayfair, and now I'm not yet ready for her to leave. Is it the way her eyes brighten when she smiles? Is it that she was still smiling when we closed the restaurant for the night?

It's too late.

We arrive at the inn without another word. The Davidson Inn is a renovated historic home. It's too dark now to make out much of the architecture, but I've seen it here all my life. I know exactly what it looks like from the wide front porch to the slate and copper roof.

It's my turn to sigh as I walk behind her up the walkway to the front of the house. *Shit.* She's limping. It's slight, but she's favoring her bad leg. Great. I didn't think of Vivienne's leg when I offered to walk her here. I only thought about wanting to spend more time with her and possibly talk her into staying longer. I should have driven her. I should not have let her work at Mayfair tonight in the first place.

Vivienne stops walking at the bottom of the steps and turns to face me. She smiles timidly.

"Thank you for giving me the chance to work for

you tonight. I know it was only one night, but I will always treasure my time here in Davidson."

"I'm the one who should thank you. Why are you thanking me?"

"I have my reasons."

"Why do you have to leave? Stay here in town a little longer. Help us until Rhonda recovers."

"I have my reasons for that, too."

"Well, I wish you would stay."

The words pop out laced with more meaning than they should have in this situation. Vivienne smiles softly.

"I wish I could."

"So, I'll mail your paycheck to the address you gave me?"

She inhales quickly. "No. That isn't necessary. Why don't you donate it to a local charity?"

"Are you sure? I know it isn't much, but you earned it."

"I'm sure. Is there an art program for children or any kind of medical charity?"

"If that's what you really want."

"I do. Thank you for handling that for me."

We stand in silence for a few long beats. I say the only thing left to say.

"Goodbye, Vivienne."

I extend my hand, and she takes it. We shake and both hold on a little longer than we should at the end. Finally, she lets go.

"Goodbye, Brady."

She turns and walks away.

I let her.

Why shouldn't I? Whether she's a biker chick or a rich heiress or both, I don't run in either of those circles. Besides, I vowed to never get involved with someone again until I get to know them first. I can't trust my heart to lead me. There have been too many instances when it's led me down the wrong path. Women who seem perfectly normal can be anything but. I've had my share of those women, the kind who take advantage of my trusting nature.

Vivienne makes no sense at all. A wealthy motorcycle mama who buys expensive gifts for strangers and acts like working at Mayfair is the most fun she's had in months. Who does that?

As curious as I am about this woman, it's a very good thing she's leaving town.

Chapter Eight

Viv

I wake up before sunrise. It was difficult to sleep, the dread of my return pushing on me as if it were an actual physical pressure. I can't put my future off any longer. Circumstances were such that I did get one extra day of life, but now I need to get an early start and make good time on my trip home. Grandmother is expecting me.

Grandmother.

She'd be so angry if she knew about me working yesterday. A Prescott wouldn't be caught dead with a menial job. We're allowed to be lawyers and occasionally run for political office—depending on which office it is. There are many rules that come with being a Prescott.

My phone chirps with a call—unusual, since the only person who has my number is Rose. I call her once a week so she knows I'm okay, but she is only to call me in emergencies.

I answer the call.

"Vivienne Elaine Prescott."

I'm pretty sure the color has immediately drained from my face, although I'm not in front of a mirror to see.

"Hello, Grandmother."

"Explain yourself."

I hold back the sigh that naturally wants to escape at this moment. That would only make Grandmother more angry.

"I'm okay, really. It was a minor accident. My bike is still running and everything."

"Not that."

"Oh, I'm on my way back home and will be there in time for the Christmas ball."

"That is not what I am referring to either." Grandmother's tone is icy.

She knows.

I'm not sure how she knows, but she does.

"I embarked on this adventure to allow myself life experiences."

"What if someone had seen you there? What were you thinking? This is scandalous."

Grandmother continues in her over-dramatic tone.

"No one will ever know. Besides, how bad would that really be? Millions of people work every day. It is nothing to be ashamed of."

"You are a Prescott, my dear. What would Henry think if he found out?"

"Henry will never find out. No one will. How did you know? How did you get my phone number?" I have to call Rose to ask if she's okay and make sure she still has a job.

"I know everything."

"Wait a minute. Did you have me followed?"

"Of course." She answers as if there is no other possibility. "I would not allow my granddaughter and heir to the Prescott fortune to go traipsing around the country unsupervised."

Anger wells up inside me. This trip was about being my own person. I'm not going to go as far as to say it was about finding myself, but who am I kidding? Of course that's what I was trying to do. I was trying to find out what it was like to *not* be a Prescott for a while. I needed a break from the duties and obligations that have suffocated me for my entire life. I wanted to be free from Grandmother these last few months. That isn't what happened.

"You've had someone watching me? For how long?"

"My people did not interfere with your trip. They only made sure you were safe. You're my granddaughter, and I love you. I couldn't let you go traipsing off into the world on your own."

It's too late to play the *I-love-you* card. That isn't what this was about at all.

"No, you wanted to be sure I didn't embarrass you or the rest of the family."

"Don't be ridiculous."

The tone of Grandmother's denial somehow confirms the opposite.

"You thought you couldn't trust me."

"How could I trust you when you were acting so unlike yourself? I needed to be sure you were safe."

"If you were so worried about my safety, then you would have called two days ago when I went to the ER. You didn't call then. Instead, you called me when you heard I was working."

"You weren't injured, not really. I saw the report. Your adventure is over, Vivienne. You stay right where you are. Rebecca will fly down later today to pick you up."

"No. I'm leaving this morning to come home on my motorcycle."

"You won't need that contraption any more. Just leave it where it is. It's time to come home."

A heavy sigh expels from deep in my chest. Years of pent-up anger swells inside me. I have always done exactly what my family expected of me. I have never let them down. I have never brought an ounce of scandal to the family name. I only asked for these last few months to be free of the Prescott chains.

"No."

"No?"

"I have changed my mind. I'm not coming home yet."

"This is not the time for impudence. You stay right where you are, and one of my people will be there to get you in a few moments."

Of course. It makes sense that if she knows where I am, she likely has someone—or maybe even more than one someone—keeping an eye on me. The last few months have been a joke. I haven't been on my own at all. I've been under Grandmother's thumb just as I've always been.

"Did you threaten Rose to get this phone number?"

"Do not change the subject, young lady."

"You did, didn't you?"

"I did no such thing. I only reminded Rose who is responsible for her paycheck."

And there it is. Grandmother wields her power with her bank account. It's her go-to for anything and everything she wants. Granted, you can certainly get a lot done when you have a balance as large as Grandmother's.

Someone could be here to get me at any moment. My packed duffel bag sits on the floor next to the bed. I add the few remaining items and slip my leathers on over my yoga pants. There's no time to lose.

"I am tired of you meddling in my life. I had every intention of coming home and performing my family duties as promised, but I have had enough. I will no longer allow you to dictate the details of my life. I have friends here who need me, and I am going to help them. Goodbye, Grandmother."

"Friends? You've been in that town for less than forty-eight hours."

Exactly what kind of updates does Grandmother get about me? Is it a morning-briefing kind of thing? Is she updated more often than that? Does she know what I ate for breakfast yesterday?

I disconnect the call, run to the bathroom for my toiletries, and grab the Mayfair uniform from the back of the chair. There's no time to lose. I quickly step into and zip up my riding boots and throw on my jacket. I close the door and rush down the stairs as quickly and quietly as possible. Lari meets me at the bottom.

"Good morning, Miss Prescott. You're up early this morning, dear."

"Good morning. I'm in a bit of a rush. Would it be possible for you to just charge the credit card I gave you yesterday?"

My credit card. Another way for Grandmother to track me. Of course I know it's possible, I just never thought she would stoop that low.

I should have known better.

"Of course, dear. I'm so sorry that you have to rush off before breakfast. May I get you a cup of coffee to go or perhaps some toast?"

"No, thank you for everything. Goodbye."

I duck out the door before Lari can delay me any

longer. Time is of the essence when dealing with Grandmother and her people. She has a way of making things happen.

I'm too late. I round the corner of the wrap-around porch to see two men loading my bike onto the back of a truck. The realization freezes me in my tracks. I've seen one of them before. He's the man from the street, the one who was staring at me from the crowd after my accident. Of course. He's one of Grandmother's minions. He nods his head in some kind of sick greeting.

Who else works for Grandmother? The doctor who saw me in the ER? Grandmother said she saw a copy of my medical report. Did Lari get a commission to keep an eye on me last night? Nothing would surprise me anymore.

I turn and walk back to the front of the inn at a normal pace. There's no reason to rush. Where would I have gone on my bike anyway? I can walk to Mayfair. Of course, Mayfair isn't open at this hour. For now, I can go to Minnie's. I turn down Elm and head toward Minnie's Diner on foot. My heavy bag feels heavier than usual, but the diner isn't far away.

I make my call on the way.

"I'm sorry, Vivienne." Rose's voice sounds rougher than usual. She's been crying.

"I'm the one who's sorry. What did she do to you?"

"She only threatened me a little bit. I still have my job and most of my dignity." Damn it. "Was it horrible for you, sweetie? Is she coming to get you?"

"No. Well, maybe. The funny thing is that I was going to come home today. Once I found out that Grandmother has had me followed during this whole trip, I decided to stay a bit longer."

Rose's gasp is audible through the phone. "That explains why she didn't try to squeeze me for your phone number before this morning. I wondered why she wasn't more worried about you. Where are you, by the way? If you aren't coming home today, what will you be doing?"

"I'm in a small town in central Virginia. Last night I worked in a restaurant." Another gasp, but this one makes me smile. "It was fun. I'm hoping I can have the job for a while. Meg and Brady need help while Rhonda is recuperating from her appendectomy."

"Who are Meg, Brady, and Rhonda?"

"Just a few of the lovely people who live here in this town."

I turn the corner onto Cherry Street and see Minnie's Diner up ahead, shining like a beacon of hope. Grandmother's men haven't tried to kidnap me off the street—not that they would make such a public spectacle, but they haven't driven by me either. They're likely hiding somewhere watching me, which they have apparently been doing this whole trip.

"You sound happier than the last few times we've spoken."

"I'm not sure if it's because I'm not coming home yet or if it's that I am finally doing something worthwhile on this trip. Either way, I do feel happier."

"I'm so glad to hear it." Rose is smiling now. I can tell. "I'll talk with you on Christmas, if not sooner. I love you, sweetie."

"Love you, too."

I disconnect with a smile. Most people don't tell their maids they love them, but since Mom and Dad died, Rose is the only person I have spoken those words to. She's been by my side during all the good and bad times in my life and is more like a grandmother to me than my own.

⁂

Minnie's is hopping this morning. It's only seven thirty and barely light outside. I recognize one friendly face immediately. Chief Tisdale.

"Well hello there, Vivienne. Care to join us for breakfast?"

He gestures to the empty seat next to him at the counter as the gentleman he's with looks up. I recognize Kate's husband right away. Luckily, he's wearing his police uniform. I don't expect Grandmother's goon to give me any real trouble, but just in case, it'll be good for him to see that I'm in good with the chief of police.

I take the empty seat next to Chief Tisdale.

"Vivienne, I believe you remember Hunter Simms?"

"Of course. Nice to see you again."

"Vivienne was our waitress at Mayfair last night."

"I heard you had a good night," Hunter replies.

"You did?"

Hunter shrugs his shoulders. His gray-green eyes seem to flash an apology. "This is a very small town. Besides Kate and Grace being worried about you, Brady's my best friend."

Melinda, the same waitress from yesterday, greets me with a cheery smile and a cup of coffee. "Biscuits and gravy again, honey, or can I get you something else this morning?"

"I would love a vegetable omelet. Do you have that?"

"Whatever you want, sweetie."

She drops a couple cream containers in front of me and moves on down the counter to pour coffee for her other patrons.

"Maybelle and I sure had fun at Mayfair last night. She wouldn't stop talking about how much she liked that bottle of champagne. That was your doing, wasn't it?"

"No, sir. That was all Brady."

"Listen here, Vivienne. I've been doing this job for more than forty years. I can spot a lie right away. I know it was you and only you responsible for that gift. If your body language didn't tell me all I needed to know, Brady's surely did. He's a horrible liar, too." Uh oh. "No worries, there. It'll be our secret, but you have to let me buy your breakfast."

"Thank you. That would be lovely."

The door opens, allowing a gust of wind to whip inside. I look up to see Grandmother's goons walk inside. They take a table somewhere behind me in the diner. Wonderful. I take out my antique compact and pretend to look at my reflection while in actuality, I pinpoint the location of the two men. They sit in a booth at the far end of the diner.

"I heard you have to leave town this morning." Hunter chimes in. "Are you just having a bite to eat before you go?"

I slip my compact back into my pocket and close the zipper. I know Grandmother won't let her men make a public display of any kind, but it still works in my favor to be sitting with two policemen. I manage a smile.

"My plans have changed, actually. I learned this morning that I can stay in town for a while after all —at least until after the holidays. I may be able to help out some more at Mayfair, if they would still like to have me. I am planning to call Meg later this morning and ask her about it."

"You can ask Brady now."

Chief Tisdale nods towards the door. I look up in time to see Brady walk through the glass door. Our eyes meet immediately. His widen in surprise at seeing me here before a smile spreads across his face. My stomach somersaults as he walks towards us.

"Vivienne, it's nice to see you. I thought you would be on the road by now."

"I was hoping to speak with you about that."

It suddenly feels like there are way too many people around. This is a public place. I had my chance to be alone with Brady last night, and the situation felt too intimate. Now that we're with Chief Tisdale and Hunter, I'd rather us be alone.

Not alone-alone. I push those thoughts out of my head. I realize I've assumed Brady would like me to work for him and fill in for Rhonda while she's recovering from her surgery. It was easy for him to make that offer when he knew I wouldn't accept it. Now, the tables have turned. I have no mode of transportation and nowhere else to go. Well, I could go back home, but I definitely don't want to do that. I'm not sure I want to go back at all after the way Grandmother treated me. I do know I don't want to go anywhere right now.

"Vivienne can stay with us a little longer." I study Brady's face as Chief Tisdale breaks the news.

"Really?"

Brady looks to me for confirmation. I nod. "My plans have changed, and if you'll have me, I would like to work at Mayfair until Rhonda can come back to work. Would that be okay?"

"Okay? That's fantastic." Brady beams now from ear to ear. "Meg'll be thrilled. She called me on the way here in a tizzy about how we're going to replace you. Only one night on staff and you made quite an impression."

"She sure made an impression with us," Chief Tisdale remarks. "Vivienne, here, is a keeper."

Chapter Nine

Brady

The chief's words replay in my mind. *Vivienne, here, is a keeper*. A big sigh escapes. Is she? A keeper, that is? She's something, although I don't know what exactly that something is.

My first instinct at seeing Vivienne here at the diner this morning was to bring her in for a tight hug. Geez, it was all I could do not to kiss her goodbye last night, which was stupid because I don't want to get involved with a woman. I'm not yet over the nightmares of my past relationships.

This will be good. Vivienne will be working at Mayfair. We don't condone relationships at work. That will help me keep the lines between us clearly drawn.

I take a seat next to Vivienne at the counter. "I'm glad you made the choice to stay here in Davidson for a while. You seemed so adamant last night that you were leaving this morning. What changed?"

She shifts in her seat uncomfortably. "I can't explain it, but suffice it to say that my prior obligations have changed, and I can stay after all." As she speaks, she turns her head away from me. A man across the room lifts his head to look at Vivienne. Their gaze holds for a couple seconds, and then she's looking back at me. The man says something to his friend and looks back at his menu.

Crap. I do like Vivienne. I like her enough that I'm imagining looks across the room that aren't even there. She knows no one in this town except for people at Mayfair and Kate. And now Chief Tisdale and Hunter, but that's only because of Mayfair. I have to stop being so paranoid.

"Whatever the reason, I'm glad your plans have changed, and you can stay here in Davidson a little longer. Does Lari have room for you at her inn?"

Vivienne shifts again on her stool. "That's a bit of a problem. Lari told me when I checked in that she only had a room for me for two nights. She's booked from now through New Year's. So, I have no place to stay."

"Yes, you do. You can stay in the apartment above the restaurant. No charge."

Her forehead furrows slightly. "Are you sure I

won't be an imposition?"

What am I doing? Torturing myself, I suppose. I've listed all the reasons that I need to stay away from Vivienne. Add to it the fact that she's now my employee, and I should be trying to keep my distance, not inviting her to stay on my property. What the hell is wrong with me?

"Not at all. There's a small apartment there, if you want to call it that. I stayed there some when we were getting Mayfair together, but no one has slept there in months. It's private, and it's yours if you want it."

"The commute would be good, especially since I no longer have my bike."

"What happened to your bike? We have a mechanic in town who can take a look at it."

Her cheeks redden. What did I say?

"A mechanic won't be necessary." Vivienne looks away for a moment before allowing her eyes to again meet mine. "I'd love to stay in the Mayfair apartment. Thank you for your kind offer."

"No, thank you. It's the least I can do since you're helping us out. I really appreciate this. Let's finish breakfast, and I'll take you over."

❖❖❖

This place looks more like a dump than I remember. Maybe because I didn't care what it looked like when I crashed here, but a beautiful heiress needs more.

I move through the room quickly, picking up odds and ends from the living area that really belong in the restaurant storage room down the hall but didn't make it there. My efforts don't help the place look better.

Vivienne sets her bag on the floor and walks over to the large window that overlooks the downtown area. The window, wood floors, and moldings are all custom and the best things about this apartment. The furnishings...not so much.

There's the cast-off living room furniture that Mom and Dad gave me when they bought new stuff over the summer. It's okay, but a bit drab since there's no artwork or anything at all to brighten up the walls. The bedroom has a bed. That's it. No dresser or nightstand or anything. I never missed having those things the few times I slept up here after a late night of working, but now it seems to matter.

Vivienne's used to much nicer furnishings, and besides, Kate would be mortified. *Kate*—exactly who I need to get over here to help me. She can work miracles with this kind of space.

I dial her number from my favorites, and she answers right away. The store doesn't open until nine o'clock, but I figure she's there getting things together for what is sure to be a crazy shopping day.

"Is Dad over there with you?"

Our father is supposed to be retired and has

turned the keys to our family's general store over to Kate. But, somehow, he always seems to make an excuse for why Kate needs his help at the store. During the holidays it makes sense, but he really just likes spending time there. Kate lets him come in whenever he wants, even though she's the one running the place these days.

"Yes, he's here." I can feel the smile on her lips. "I welcome the help. It's Christmas Eve eve. I think we'll be super-busy today."

"Yeah, probably. Can you help me with something for a little while? It's kind of important. I'm in the apartment above Mayfair."

Is it important? It feels like it. I can't let Vivienne stay here with this place looking like this. I wanted to be the person who saved the day for her, since she has totally saved it for me. Looking around this place doesn't make it seem like much of a gift at this point.

"Sure, I'll be right over."

"Why does Kate need to come?"

I feel the embarrassment hit my cheeks. "I think it's best if she helps me whip this place into shape. I didn't realize how bad it really is." Vivienne probably lives with chandeliers and servants. "I can't let you stay here with it looking like this."

"Not at all. It's lovely. I can spend some time today tidying the place up. I don't have anything else to do anyway."

"Let Kate help. She lives for this kind of thing."

❖❖❖

"I barely recognize the place. How did you make such a drastic change in such a short amount of time?"

"It's what I do," Kate announces with a smug grin.

It's true. My sister is gifted at transforming a place from drab to fab in an hour. I swear a blog isn't enough for her to showcase her talents. She should have her own television show.

"I thought I'd come back and find you'd painted the room a different color." I've only been gone a couple hours, but you never know with Kate, and repainting is her usual go-to for sprucing a place up.

She did make some changes, although none of them drastic. There's a colorful blanket on the back of the couch and light green curtains hanging from the small window in the kitchen. The large picture window remains uncovered. I like it better this way.

"Wait until you see the bedroom."

I follow my sister into the small bedroom. My mouth hangs open in surprise. A large oak dresser takes up almost the entire wall across from the bed. A mirror is propped on top, waiting to be hung on the wall. Two matching nightstands with lamps flank the queen-sized bed that's been there all along, but it looks brighter with the blue quilt that covers it.

Vivienne stands next to the bed, fluffing a pillow.

She places it on the bed and smiles at me. Her leather clothes have been replaced with jeans and a light pink t-shirt. I like this soft look. My stomach flips. Yeah, I like it a lot.

"How did you manage to pull all this together so quickly?"

"Granny was just telling me the other day she wanted to get rid of this furniture, but she didn't know who to give it to. Hunter and Bryce were having a slow police day, so they had time to move it here for us.

The linens came from my stock. There are a few other odds and ends we had to get from the store. I'll send you a bill for those." I roll my eyes. Kate and Vivienne just laugh. "Mom's bringing over a microwave and a coffee pot. You're lucky she had them, or I'd have to charge you the big bucks for those."

Kate steps back and takes a photo of the finished bedroom. "It didn't take long, and I'm glad to do it. Now I have some new material for my blog. I haven't been as regular about posting as I used to be, and everything I've done the last two months has been holiday-related. It's nice to have a little break.

We can come back after the first of the year and paint this room a pale blue that matches this."

Kate points to one of the small flowers repeated in the design of the quilt. That would be really nice. It's too bad we don't have the opportunity to do that for Vivienne before she moves in.

"I honestly don't know how to thank you both for this. I don't know the last time someone did something so nice for me."

"You've been a big help to Brady and Meg, and besides that, I'm really having fun getting to know you."

Kate and Vivienne share a smile.

Chapter Ten

Viv

Brady steps close to Kate and pulls her in for a hug. Kate lets him. I can only imagine the concept of a sibling. It isn't the first time I've had these kinds of feelings. Being an only child can feel lonely sometimes, especially now with Mom and Dad gone. But, it is the first time I've seen a brother and sister willingly embrace for no reason other than that they actually feel love and thankfulness for each other.

My cousins never came close to this kind of affection. They would only hug each other if one or both of them would get some kind of benefit out of the action. That's typical for my family. All Grandmother has to do is wave the carrot of the family fortune over them, and they'll do whatever she wants.

People at home do nice things for me all the time but for the wrong reasons. They want Grandmother to notice their actions or perhaps other people to notice that they're spending time with a Prescott.

Henry's family has plenty of money, yet he knows if he marries me, he will get more. *More. More. More.* Henry will never have enough money or power to suit him. At least I was able to decide that much on this trip. I may have to eventually take my parents' place at the foundation and do Grandmother's bidding, but I will not marry Henry simply for the sake of creating a family tie with his. I'm holding out hope that Grandmother has changed her mind about that part of her plan, and if she hasn't, then I will have to change it for her.

Henry hasn't asked me to marry him—not yet anyway. It's just another one of Grandmother's plans to bring our families together. I know Henry will be all for it, but our future would be nothing but misery all around. I have to draw the line there. I refuse to marry anyone for the sake of some family political connection.

Brady and Kate are so thoughtful. They went through all of this effort to make me comfortable just because I needed a place to stay. Sure, I'm helping Brady out at the restaurant, but they didn't have to go this overboard.

They're doing all this work simply because

they're nice people and not because they want to get in my good graces. For all they know, I'm some crazy woman who travels around the country on my bike, doing nice things for people out of the kindness of my heart. The thought brings tears to my eyes.

"Hey, are you okay?" Brady squeezes my shoulder. Our eyes meet as I come out of my thoughts. "You look a little dazed."

"I was just caught up in the kindness of your gesture." Brady's still touching me. In addition to the warmth, my shoulder is beginning to tingle. *Keep it together.*

"I raised them to be kind. They know I'll still take them over my knee if they're anything else."

Grace's expression is stern, but the love in her eyes shines through clear as can be. She gives Brady a quick hello hug and then turns to me. I hold my hand out for a shake. Grace latches onto it and then pulls me in for a warm hug. I come up for air and see Brady beaming down at us.

How are these people so nice?

"We hug our hellos here. Very nice to see you again, Viv. I do hope Brady's been taking good care of you."

"Yes ma'am."

I catch my first glimpse of the pattern on the t-shirt Grace wears under her red cardigan sweater. It's a picture of Elvis Presley wearing a Santa hat. My mouth opens in shock, but I quickly close it and smile.

"I see by your expression that you've noticed Mom's colorful attire." Brady puts his arm around Grace's shoulders and smiles. "She has an unhealthy obsession with Elvis, and most of her wardrobe pieces declare it to the world."

"Elvis is 'the King' for a reason. Besides, it's my life. I should be able to wear whatever I wish. The older I've gotten, the more I've realized I only have myself to please, but after the cancer, I find the sentiment more true than ever."

"Cancer? I'm so sorry to hear it."

Brady's no longer smiling.

"No worries, sweetie. I'm kicking its butt."

"The cancer didn't stand a chance against Mom," Kate comments with a bit of a forced chuckle.

Brady leans in and kisses his mom on her head.

"Alright, I brought up the coffee pot. Brady, you go grab the microwave and the groceries from my car."

"You bought me groceries?"

I feel my eyes moisten with tears. Grace takes my hand and squeezes it. "Just a few basics, sweetie. Kate said we needed to get you set up in this apartment. We don't half-ass anything we do."

My morning flies by. My new little apartment was set up by eleven o'clock. Grace left soon after she arrived, but she wouldn't go until I promised to join their family for Christmas dinner. I can hardly imagine a Christmas different than the ones I've had my whole life. Yet, here I am in this little town with new friends who were strangers only two days ago.

Kate and Grace, especially, were insistent about my spending Christmas with them. Brady didn't seem against the idea exactly, but he didn't threaten to have Kate's husband, Hunter, bring me there in handcuffs if I don't join them like his mother did.

Kate and Brady went back to work just after eleven o'clock. I spent some time lounging and getting used to my new place. At least thirty minutes of that time was spent standing next to the window memorizing the details of the Richardson General Store across the street.

The building takes up a huge part of the block where Main Street and Cherry Street come together. In the first ten minutes, my eyes were always brought back to the store window. It's a sight to behold for sure. Colorful lights shine from within to brighten this dull day. I can't quite make out much of what else is inside from this angle, but there's a lot of red and white in there.

After getting my fill of the store window, I was able to concentrate on the structure of the building itself. It is far from a brick rectangle. The brickwork is quite detailed with a pattern that is repeated across the top of the building and under the windows and quoined corners.

The urge to paint fills me, something I haven't

felt for months, not since Mom and Dad passed away. I was hoping this trip of mine would bring back my love for painting, but those feelings remained buried deep inside me until right now.

I run to my bag and remove my paints. What I don't have is something to paint on. I wasted the two small canvases I had during forced painting sessions in the Smokey Mountains. Kate said they sell everything at her store. Could they really sell blank canvases?

There's only one way to find out. I don my leather coat and head out the door of my apartment, down the stairs to Mayfair, and out the back door into the small alley. This is the same way I came out with Brady last night when we walked to the inn.

Things were sure different then. I thought that would be the last time I saw Brady, and instead of leaving town, I'm now living—albeit temporarily—above his restaurant.

A sigh escapes me as I turn the corner.

I stop in my tracks.

Grandmother's minion is standing on the sidewalk, a cup of coffee in his hand. His eyes widen at the sight of me but quickly regain their shape before he smiles and tips his paper cup at me.

My surprise is short-lived as it soon morphs into anger. I walk directly to him.

"What is your name?"

"Gerard." He sticks out his arm as if he means to shake hands. I have no intention of sharing social niceties with this man. He figures that out for himself and then pulls his arm back toward his body.

"Gerard, you can leave now."

His smile takes on a creepy quality. He shrugs. "We both know that isn't going to happen."

He's right. He's following Grandmother's orders. She's the person I have to convince. I walk down the rest of the block to the crosswalk and take out my phone. I can't live like this anymore.

Grandmother doesn't answer. Instead, I hear the raspy voice of her assistant, Rebecca. The forced sweetness of her voice makes me cringe.

"Vivienne, dear, is that you? I've been so worried about you."

Rebecca has worked for my grandmother for as long as I can remember. She's never been married and never had children. She sacrificed that kind of life to be Grandmother's well-paid go-to girl. She does her job very well. Her worry for me is completely manufactured. She likely just got a call from the guy who's spying on me reporting my every move.

"Has this man been watching me for my entire trip?"

"No, he's fairly new."

"But someone has been watching me the whole time, right?"

"Your grandmother loves you. She was beside herself with worry when you left. She needed reassurance that you were safe. That's all. They never intervened. She was so worried when you took that tumble on your motorcycle."

Yet, she didn't call then to see how I was doing. Instead, she called to yell at me about working at Mayfair.

"Look, Rebecca. I'm safe. You know where I am now, and I assure you I'm not going anywhere until after New Year's when I will come straight home. So, would you please ask Grandmother to call off these guys?"

Home. Home is supposed to be a place of warmth and comfort where a person is free to be themselves. Manningsgate is none of these things. With each passing day, I want to go *home* less and less. How can I possibly get out of it?

I sigh and take in the festive window of the general store from ground level. It's breathtaking, really. Colorful lights outline the frame. Red stockings with white and gold trim hang along the base of the window.

What's going on inside is breathtaking. White fabric has been laid in the base of the window to look like snow. A vintage sled and ice skates are placed around an impressive Christmas tree. It's a live tree decorated with clear, twinkling lights.

It's covered with the most amazing ornaments. Roughly half of them are copper cut-outs in various Christmas shapes, which appear to be hand-cut and hand-pounded. The raw edges give the copper more places to glow. The other half of the ornaments are blown-glass balls in varying sizes in either light blue or clear glass. The entire picture is spectacular.

"Vivienne, did you hear me?"

"It must be a bad connection." Or I was too enthralled by the glow of the window display. "What did you say?"

Rebecca doesn't sigh or show any sign that she's unhappy having to repeat herself. Still, I can feel her displeasure. She has no right to be so snooty to me, but she's spent enough time with Grandmother that she's taken on her air of superiority.

"It's true that Mrs. Prescott is very concerned about your recent employment. I didn't believe it at first myself. What would make you want to take a job as a waitress?"

This conversation is useless. The person I have to convince is Grandmother. There's little benefit in hashing this out with Rebecca.

"I don't want to talk about this right now. Please give Grandmother my message and ask her to call me so we can discuss this issue. Goodbye."

I disconnect and sneak a look at Grandmother's goon. The jerk is still smiling. I wish I hadn't looked because the anger fills my insides. I take a deep breath and will it away. Davidson is a happy place.

With a heavy sigh, I push the door to enter the general store. A little bell over my head jingles to announce my arrival.

"What's that sad face for? Everything okay over there?"

Kate walks towards me wearing a concerned look. I shake off the feelings of Grandmother's interference and do my best to concentrate on why I'm here.

"I'm fine. I just really need some painting canvases. Do you sell anything like that?"

"We have a few—no big sizes or anything. Come with me, and I'll show you."

I let Kate lead the way and take in the sights of the store. There are so many things to see. The first section is full of sweets. We walk down a long aisle with shelves of candy on both sides. It seems as if every kind of candy is represented. My world gets bigger when we step out of the aisle into an open area filled with barrels and bins filled with even more candy: chocolate-covered nuts, fruit candies, gummy candies.

"This place is incredible."

Kate smiles. "The soda fountain is my favorite part of the whole store."

She gestures to the left, and I understand what she means. It's right out of an old movie. The long stainless steel counter is at least twenty feet long. Red-topped stools line the outside to provide seating. There are many glass jars filled with candy toppings and a large neon red sign. A couple sits together at one end of the counter enjoying chocolate milkshakes.

"Wow, I see what you mean. It looks too perfect to be real."

"My grandfather installed the soda counter back in the forties. We've tried very hard to keep it authentic over the years.

The art supplies are right over here. We keep a few things stocked for a local woman who teaches art classes."

The largest size Kate has is eight by ten inches. I choose four of the canvases and two paint brushes, which are surprisingly good quality for a small-town store that also sells horse feed. It is abundantly clear that this is not your usual shop. There's something here for everyone.

"How do you keep stock of so many items?"

Kate shrugs. "It's a matter of knowing what my clients need. Many people in Davidson prefer to buy local, and they do. So, I stock whatever it is they need to buy."

"This place is wonderful. I'm excited to get back, so I can paint for a couple hours before Mayfair opens."

"Well, let's get to it."

I pay for my purchases and rush back across the street, ignoring my babysitter, Gerard. He gives me a nod and sits down on a bench as if he's just someone enjoying an afternoon cup of coffee. I do my best to shrug off the bad feelings associated with him. I'm about to paint, finally, and I don't want anything getting in the way.

Brady pokes his head out of the office when I walk into Mayfair.

"What are you up to this afternoon?"

"I'm just getting back from the general store." I say with a huge grin on my face. "It's an amazing place."

"It is."

"See you in a few hours."

Brady doesn't say anything else, which is great because I'm already moving up the stairs. The urge to begin is practically pulling me along. Once inside my little apartment, I slide my jacket off and let it fall to the floor. I know exactly what I'm going to paint, and it's like I cannot get to it fast enough.

I get set up at the window using the ledge to prop up my canvas. It isn't ideal, but it works well enough. It feels like my soul sighs with relief with the first stroke of my brush.

I'm painting again.

Finally.

When I'd set out on my journey last June, I thought I would be painting often. I pictured myself living in the moment so I could just pull to the side of the road on a whim and paint a pretty view or anything that struck my fancy.

That never happened. The urge to paint buried itself deep inside me. I did try to paint a couple times while visiting the Smoky Mountains. The views of the mountains were quite heavenly, but I couldn't get the images in my brain on the canvas. I stood in my spot for more than an hour trying to get the motivation. Inspiration was all around me, but besides a few forced strokes, the canvas remained empty.

Not today. The brush moves smoothly, as if I have not had months away from my favorite activity. I smile to myself as the image becomes clearer. Life is good.

Chapter Eleven

Brady

Vivienne's hanging in there, but her performance isn't as good as it was last night. It's been mostly little issues like when she forgot to bring bread to two of her tables, and they had to ask for it. I pretended not to notice, but it clearly bothered Vivienne.

There was one grumpy man from out of town who insisted he ordered his filet medium, and it was cooked too done for him. I did get involved with that one. It was a well-done steak. Vivienne insisted that's what he ordered. Based on the expression on the face of the man's wife, he was at fault, but per our policy, we made the man a new steak. He seemed somewhat satisfied after I gave them each a free dessert. That's likely what he was after all along. This kind of thing happens from time to time, but the situation really seemed to fluster Vivienne. She isn't the same chipper employee she was after her first shift. Tonight, she looks exhausted.

I run the check for Vivienne's last guests. They gave her a thirty percent tip. Leo and Katherine don't usually get tipped this much, so Vivienne must be doing something right.

"Now that's a good way to end the night."

She gives me a small smile in return, but that's all. Manny is all about the tips. He holds the record for the highest percentage and amount. Despite Vivienne's occasional errors, she's likely to beat that record. Her wine sales continue to be impressive.

"Is there anything else I need to do down here? I think I'm going to call it a night."

I rack my brain, trying to come up with something I might need Vivienne's help with. Mostly to spend more time with her. Nothing comes to mind, and while I'm happy she's living upstairs now, that means I don't get to walk her home like I did last night.

"You can go."

"Goodnight."

She walks into the small hallway that connects to the stairs, office, and back door. I follow.

"Vivienne, you okay?"

She stops and leans against the wall. "Just tired, I

think. This has been a very long day."

Our eyes meet, and I see the exhaustion there. "You did fine tonight. I don't expect you to be perfect, you know."

"You and your family have been so nice to me. I want to be good enough to deserve it."

Wait. Is that...?

Shit. One single tear falls. I bring my hand close and wipe it gently away. Vivienne doesn't retreat, so I leave my hand there in case another one follows. Or, it could be because her skin is so soft, and I don't want to stop touching her.

"You don't need to worry about deserving anything. You already do. Just be yourself. Everyone loves you."

"Hey, Brady." Meg's words are cut off. My hand flies away from Vivienne's cheek. "I'm so sorry. We'll talk later." Meg disappears back into the kitchen.

"Goodnight, Brady." Vivienne doesn't wait for a response before she turns and disappears up the stairs.

✣✣✣

"Don't say a word. That wasn't what it looked like."

Meg turns her lips inward in an effort to stifle her smile. She's unsuccessful.

"You should go for it. Viv's really nice."

"I know nothing about her." Okay, that's not

exactly true. I know enough about her that she makes *no* sense whatsoever.

"*Get to know her*. There are some people who put off a good vibe. Viv's one of them. You're attracted to her, right?" I roll my eyes in response. How are we even having this conversation? "Yeah, of course you are. She's gorgeous."

"She's also my employee."

"*Temporary* employee."

"Whatever. She still works here."

Meg tilts her head to the side. "Don't overthink everything. Just go with it and see what happens." A sigh escapes me. My chest still feels heavy. "What do you know about her?"

"She likes good wine—like really good wine, and she says the names of the vineyards in French."

She's also totally loaded. I can't say that part out loud. When I did the internet search on Vivienne, it was only to protect Mayfair. I had to know if she was a crazy person who would murder our guests or run off with their credit cards. While I feel justified that the internet search was for our own protection, there's a part of me that feels guilty for executing it in the first place. Knowing about her wealth is becoming more like a secret I wish I didn't have.

"Is that a bad thing?" The words bring me back to our conversation.

"No, but it doesn't jive with the fact that she rides a motorcycle from place to place. Who does that?"

Meg wrinkles her nose and then full-on frowns.

"Don't judge. You don't know what kind of life she's led. You know, I came to Davidson under mysterious circumstances, and you still trusted me."

True. When I met Meg, she was in Davidson hiding from someone who wanted her dead. I've never once considered Meg to be a criminal, even though I could have easily come to that conclusion.

"I just don't want to take the risk and end up being a fool again. How many times do I have to fall for the wrong woman before it stops blowing up in my face?"

"As many times as it takes to find the right one. Just don't rush into anything. Take your time. Get to know Viv."

"She won't be here long enough for that. She's only in town until Rhonda comes back to work in January."

Meg shrugs. "What's meant to be will be. Just let it happen, and don't stress about it."

Easier said than done.

Chapter Twelve

Viv

The frosty air outside makes it feel like Christmas Eve, but my plans for the day couldn't be farther from my norm.

This is the day of the Prescott Christmas Ball. For my entire life and then some, Grandmother has thrown the party of the century on this night, and I've always attended. When I was really young, I would only be allowed to make an appearance before being swept away by Rose. This party is where I had my first real dance, my first glass of champagne, and my first taste of the lengths to which people will go in order to further their own agendas.

I remember the first time I learned this harsh reality. Arthur Manchester first started talking to me around Halloween. He paid me compliments every day. He asked to sit with me at lunch. I was only a freshman and hadn't dated at all. Arthur was a senior, and he was so cute. I thought it was love for sure.

When December came around, I invited him to the Christmas Ball. He looked incredibly handsome in his tuxedo. We danced a total of three dances. Arthur spent most of the evening speaking with other guests.

At the end of the evening, he thanked me for the invitation and never asked to have lunch with me again. Arthur got what he had wanted from me. I gave him the opportunity to network with important people. He went on to intern for Senator Monroe that summer, a connection made at Grandmother's party.

That experience had completely opened my eyes. It was the first time I realized how manipulative and greedy some people can be to get what they want. Everyone wants something. That's why people have relationships. Whether it is as friends or lovers, there's something to be given and received by both parties.

Tonight, I will spend my Christmas Eve working at Mayfair. Strangely, it feels better than attending the party. The people I've met here in Virginia are kinder and more genuine than the people I grew up with. They don't know that being associated with me could have any major advantage to them. That works for me.

The ring of my phone brings me out of my thoughts. *Rebecca*. I consider not answering the call, but there's no point in that. She'll just call back or worse, send my babysitter in here to get me. With a huge sigh, I connect the call.

"Good morning, Rebecca."

"I'm downstairs. Would you please let me in before I freeze to death?"

"Downstairs, as in you flew to Virginia?"

"Yes. Now, please let me inside, so that I can do what I came here to do."

"What is that, exactly?"

"Talk you into coming home with me today."

"That is not going to happen. I am planning to stay here for as long as my friends need me to be here."

"You have to hear me out. We both know I must execute your grandmother's orders. Now let me in."

"I will be right down."

I pull on yoga pants and quickly slip into a bra. I need to be at least somewhat presentable. I run my fingers through my hair while I wait for the coffee to start brewing. That will have to do.

I breathe in a huge sigh, walk down the stairs, and open the back door. Rebecca stands in the alley, looking completely out of place. She wears a long dress coat that falls to her shins. She wears tall brown boots. Her hair is pulled back into a tight bun, her usual hairstyle, which has always reminded me of her personality. There's nothing soft about Rebecca.

She gives me a once-over with her beady, brown eyes, clearly not pleased with what she sees. Honestly, it's before eight o'clock in the morning. If I were at home, I would be expected to be fully dressed before accepting a visitor. But, I'm not at home.

"How did you know where I was? To come to the back door?"

Rebecca lifts her eyebrows. Yeah, that was kind of a dumb question.

I gesture to the very large suitcase at her side. "Are you planning on staying a while?"

"Not at all. These are your things. Rose asked me to bring them. Please do not tell your grandmother."

Really? Rebecca doing something nice for me that is clearly against Grandmother's wishes? This can't be happening.

"Are you going to invite me inside, or have you lost all of your manners?"

"Of course. Please do come in." I step to the side to allow Rebecca entry. She rolls the suitcase into the small hallway. I take it from her, and she lets me. "Right up these stairs here." Rebecca goes on ahead while I struggle to bring the suitcase up with me. It's very heavy, but I manage.

Rebecca is silent when she steps inside my little

apartment. She studies every part of the living area with her eagle eyes.

"*This* is where you are staying?"

Back to the old Rebecca, I see. I don't know where she comes off being so snobby. This place isn't much smaller than her own apartment in our family home at Manningsgate. Maybe my little apartment isn't as nicely appointed as the servant quarters there, but it comes with less of a price tag.

Rebecca is still looking at me, waiting for a response.

"Yes, this place is quaint and comfortable. I like being here." Her expression doesn't change. "Would you like some coffee?"

"No, thank you. I don't expect to be here long. It's a busy day at home, as you know, and I have many duties I must complete to prepare for the ball this evening."

"Okay."

"Please tell me about these friends you spoke of. Are they Brady Richardson and Meg McMann?"

My mouth opens. I clamp it closed before I say something I may regret. Of course Grandmother has checked out the people who own Mayfair.

"Yes, Brady and Meg are two of my new friends here in town." I hold my breath, waiting for Rebecca to reveal whatever intelligence she's uncovered about them.

"Are you enjoying your work as a waitress?"

I stand a little taller. "As a matter of fact, I am. I

find it quite fulfilling."

"I want to help you, Vivienne, but what am I to tell your grandmother about why I couldn't bring you back with me?"

Why is Rebecca so helpful all of a sudden? If I can get her to leave, then I'll have plenty of time to ponder that question later. Right now, I need to focus.

"You should tell Grandmother the truth. I want to find out who I am, other than being a Prescott."

"I can't tell her that."

I bite my lip. Rebecca's right. Grandmother would never understand why I'd want to be anything except a Prescott. I shrug. I have nothing else, and I'm not going to lie. Besides the fact that I make it a practice never to lie, I am not going to cheapen my experience here.

"Maybe she won't understand, but that's the truth." Rebecca nods and turns toward the door. That's it? "Why are you letting me off the hook so easily?"

"Patrick spoke to me as I was leaving this morning. He understands your wish to get away for a while and asked me to give you a little more time in your endeavor, if that is what you truly wish."

Uncle Patrick? Why would Rebecca listen to anything Uncle Patrick has to say, especially regarding me? Grandmother runs everything. Uncle Patrick is usually there, getting handouts for his family and nothing more. Rebecca, however, is not the person to ask about this.

"That was very kind of Uncle Patrick. I'm glad he understands my need to have a little more time to myself." We walk together in silence down the stairs and to the back door. "Please give Grandmother my love, and Merry Christmas to you, Rebecca."

"Merry Christmas to you as well, Vivienne. Good luck celebrating the holiday in this place."

"Bless you, Rose. You are the best."

I speak the words out loud after I've opened the suitcase. Rose thinks of everything. She knew that if I'm staying here in Davidson for a while, I would need some essentials. She sent a sample of what's in my closet at home: jeans, dress slacks, two dresses, sweaters, blouses, and two pair of shoes that will go with everything. She even packed a purse, makeup, and a winter coat.

I've been traveling light and without many of the items that at home would be necessities—a pair of jeans, one pair of yoga pants, a sweater, three t-shirts, and no makeup at all.

At the very bottom of the suitcase I find a tiny, wrapped box. A Christmas gift. I open it to find a small oval piece of metal engraved with the words *Be true to yourself.*

Rose knows me better than anyone left on this earth. I give her a call to tell her so. She begins work at seven o'clock each morning, so I know she's awake this early. I speak into the phone as soon as she answers.

"Thank you so much for sending the clothes and other things. As usual, you knew exactly what I needed."

"You're welcome, sweetie."

"And the Christmas gift as well. I have something for you, but I didn't think to give it to Rebecca to bring to you." And even if I had remembered, it may never have made it to Rose.

"How did it go with the Queen of Cold?"

"Somehow, it was okay. Rebecca expressed Grandmother's wish that I come home with her, but she didn't push me at all. She said that Uncle Patrick understands why I am away and wants me to have all the time I need."

"Really?"

"Strange, right?"

"Yes, very strange. Since when does Rebecca care what Mr. Prescott thinks?"

"My thoughts exactly. I've never seen Rebecca sway from Grandmother's wishes."

"I will see what I can find out about that. Merry Christmas, sweetheart."

We disconnect the call, and I spend some time leisurely unpacking the suitcase while enjoying a cup of coffee.

I jump at the sound of a knock. My hand flies to my chest. Why am I so jumpy? It can't be just anyone. It has to be someone with a key to Mayfair. I giggle to myself as I walk to my apartment door.

"Viv, it's Kate. Are you awake?" My smile grows as I turn the handle and open the door. Kate stands in the entryway carrying a pink and white pastry box. She raises the box a few inches and executes a partial bow. "Breakfast is served." With a chuckle, she walks inside, places the items on the small kitchen bar, and opens the box. "Leslie's makes amazing pastries. I hope you like them."

I select a pear tart and place it on a napkin. Kate chooses a plain croissant. She declines coffee and opts for a glass of water instead. We sit together on the small couch. I realize that I don't know Kate very well at all, but sitting here with her in my little apartment, as the morning sun filters through the large window, feels cozy and secure.

Madison is my best friend at home. She would never arrive bearing breakfast, and if she ever did, I would wonder what she was up to. I have none of those suspicions right now with Kate.

"This is lovely. The generosity of your family continues to amaze me."

Kate smiles again. "You're very sweet. Truthfully, I'm being totally selfish. I was having a hankering for a Leslie's croissant—these pregnancy cravings are not easy—so I thought it would be easier to justify the treat if I had a partner in crime."

I take a bite of the tart. It's almost as good as the little pâtisserie we visit when we're in St. Remy.

"Will you have a busy day at the store today with last-minute shoppers and all that?"

Kate nods. "Business is usually pretty busy on Christmas Eve. We close at five o'clock this afternoon, so people have to get their shopping finished early."

"Do you and Hunter have any special plans this evening?"

"We do." Her hand moves to her belly. "I'm making Hunter Frito Chili Pie for dinner, and then for dessert, we're going to open the envelope from Dr. Messing to find out the gender of our baby." Kate's eyes tear up a little when she speaks.

"What a special moment. I have to ask though, what is Frito Chili Pie?"

"You haven't lived until you've had it. I'll make it for you sometime." She takes a thoughtful sip of her water. "Maybe I can have you and Brady over for dinner before you leave."

Me and Brady?

Before I can open my mouth to contradict her, Kate begins speaking. "I don't mean as a couple. I mean just as adults and friends. You are both adults and friends, right?"

"Yes, to the adults part. I'm not sure if we're friends. Sometimes Brady seems to like me well enough, but other times it seems as if he would rather speak with anyone else."

Kate pops up to sit a bit straighter.

"Has he been rude to you?"

"Oh, no. Not at all. Brady's been very kind. He let me move in here, so I would have a place to stay while I'm in town. He has been very welcoming, I suppose." Kate tilts her head to the side and looks at me. "It is in his looks. Sometimes they're so intense, like he's studying me, and he doesn't smile very much when I'm around."

Kate nods a few times and purses her lips. "It's not his fault exactly. Brady has trust issues."

"He mentioned it to me before. Was it really that bad?"

"Brady's had some pretty rotten luck in the love department. The women he's fallen for in the past haven't been the best choices for him."

"Do you mean your family didn't approve of his past girlfriends?"

"I wish it were that simple. Brady went on two dates with a woman from Charlottesville before he learned she was married."

"Married? How awful."

"Yeah. He found out when he got an angry call from her husband. Apparently, she was using Brady to get her husband's attention. People are so strange." I shake my head and try to imagine what Brady would have felt like at receiving the news. He's clearly a noble man. Why would someone do that to him? "That isn't the worst example." Kate continues. "The woman Brady dated last fall turned out to be a diamond smuggler."

"What?"

"It's true. Brady dated her for a couple of months and had no idea of her criminal dealings. It turned out she targeted him from the beginning because he's such a nice guy, and she needed someone to unwittingly help her.

"Brady was hurt, and it could have turned out so much worse. Brady and I were both kidnapped as part of that whole ordeal, and Kennedy and I were held at gunpoint." I feel my jaw drop open and don't bother closing it. That is a perfectly legitimate response, considering what Kate just told me. "Fortunately, that's the worst example, but Brady has been hurt by other women as well."

How many women? My stomach burns. Why do I even care? I was just commenting that I'm not sure if Brady and I are even friends, and now I'm jealous?

I know it has something to do with our moment in the hallway last night. My cheek still feels tingly where Brady caressed it. The memory pops me back into the here and now where I find Kate studying me with raised eyebrows and pursed lips.

"What?" It's all I can say to diffuse her attention.

"Nothing."

It doesn't feel like nothing, but if I tell her there is nothing romantic between me and Brady, she'll see it as a sign that there might eventually be something between us. And there won't be. Kate saves me from any further discussion and quickly stands.

"I have to get going. I didn't plan to stay here this long."

I stand as well and walk Kate to the door. “Have a wonderful time tonight. I’m very excited for you and Hunter. Do you have a preference for a girl or a boy?”

“I’m good either way. Hunter would like a girl, but I don’t think he’d be devastated if we had a boy.”

She gives me a long goodbye hug. I am so thankful fate brought me here to Davidson, Virginia.

Chapter Thirteen

Brady

This woman is impossible. I don't know whether to embrace Vivienne or run away from her. My own mother has chosen to hug her apparently. I watch with a shake of my head as Mom pulls Vivienne to her. Vivienne smiles and returns the gesture. Mom insisted she and Dad be sat in Vivienne's section tonight.

Typical Mom. She wants to bring everyone into her fold. She's too trusting and immediately thinks the best of people. Maybe that's where I get it from. I used to trust everyone, but not anymore. I've learned that people lie, and it's not always easy to tell the good from the bad.

Vivienne doesn't seem bad at all. In fact, she seems amazing. That's the problem. How can I try to keep my distance from this woman when my family keeps bringing her closer? Never mind the fact that I'm the one who invited Vivienne to stay in the apartment upstairs. That gesture was a temporary moment of insanity and has nothing to do with the fact that I'm dying to know what she tastes like when I kiss her.

Why am I doing this to myself? The dread nags at the recesses of my brain. I know what's coming if I let myself get wrapped up in this woman. Why is it that after all I've been through with the opposite sex, I'm still dying to be with Vivienne? She's going to leave in a couple weeks. It's not enough time to get to know her.

Her short time in Davidson could be a good thing. There's no pressure. No strings. We could be together, and then when Vivienne's time here is up, she can leave without either of us feeling heartbroken.

It's never that simple, though. Every smile she sends me chips away at the wall I've built around my heart. It's taken more than a year to fortify myself from this very thing, and apparently it hasn't worked. I knew I was in trouble the moment she took that helmet off. Still, I don't have to give up without a fight.

Geez, Hunter would laugh at me if he heard my internal dialogue right now. Fortifying my heart?

Shit, I sound like a lovesick wimp. I'm definitely not letting go easily.

"You'll give Viv a ride to the cabin for Christmas tomorrow, won't you?"

Mom gives me a goodbye hug now, although it isn't as tight or as long as the one she gave Vivienne.

"Of course. I won't let her walk."

With Dad, it's a quick hug combined with a slap on the back.

"Make sure you let Viv know. I didn't say anything to her yet, since I hadn't talked to you about it."

Mom's eyes twinkle, and the shine has nothing to do with the Christmas lights we hung around the dining room.

Wait a minute.

"You're not trying to matchmake, are you?"

Mom waves her hand in my direction and lets it fall. "Of course not." *Right.* "The woman needs a ride. I want to be sure she gets one."

Mom looks as innocent as can be. I'm not buying it.

"We know nothing about this woman, you know. She could be the Christmas Slayer and wanted in ten states. She worms her way into strangers' lives, hoping for an invitation to Christmas dinner, and then she kills them all with the carving knife."

Mom's jaw drops. Her fingers wrap around my forearm before pulling me out the door and into the cold night. *Uh-oh.* She lets the door close behind us and stands for a moment, hands on hips, as if either she isn't yet sure what to say, or she has to dampen her anger before she can form words.

"I raised you better than that, young man." Yeah, it's the anger one. Mom's good and mad. "Vivienne's a beautiful, smart, and caring young woman. She stayed here in Davidson to help *you* in your time of need. Why would you say such a thing?"

Because I know she's keeping secrets. She hasn't told anyone about her wealth. What else is she hiding?

"Why did she stay? Has she given you an answer to that question? One minute, she has to hop on that flipping Harley of hers and ride home immediately, and there's no talking her into staying. The next minute, her bike has suddenly disappeared, and she's moved into my apartment."

Mom's cheeks are red, possibly from the cold. I'm going to go with that.

"You invited Viv to stay in that apartment, and you helped her move in."

"There are things about her we don't know."

"Of course there are. We've only known the woman a few days. I'm not adding her to my will; I simply invited her to Christmas dinner. She has no one here, and there is no way on God's green earth I'm letting that sweet girl spend Christmas alone. Now, you get back in there, offer her a ride to the cabin tomorrow, and thank her for staying here to help you for the holidays."

I'll get no help from Dad, who stands frozen with his forehead furrowed and his mouth pressed into a thin line.

Besides, Mom's right. I'm expecting too much from Vivienne. I have only known her for four days. There's something about her that's exciting and new. There's also the warmth I feel in the pit of my stomach when she looks at me with those caramel eyes.

I like her—someone I barely know—and that's my issue to deal with. Other than some occasional appreciation for a woman I've seen here or there, I haven't liked anyone since Jamie. The Jamie-nightmare was more than a year ago, but the effects of our *relationship* have haunted me ever since. There's nothing like being kidnapped and finding out your girlfriend had been using you to help her smuggle diamonds to put you off dating women forever.

Is it time to try again? I'll have to figure my love life out later because Mom is waiting for my answer.

"Yes, ma'am."

She looks at me with those light blue eyes that seem more like steel when she's upset or angry. She's clearly suspicious about my change of tone.

"You best not show up tomorrow without Viv."

"Yes, ma'am."

"And treat her kindly tonight. It's Christmas Eve, and she's alone."

I pull Mom in for another hug. "Yes, ma'am," I say

quietly.

"I love you, Brady."

"You too, Mom."

✣✣✣

"Merry Christmas."

These are my first words to Vivienne when she opens the door on Christmas Day, and just like that, I've already crossed one item off Mom's requirement list.

I'm not sure what I expected, but the woman in front of me isn't it. Her hair is down—no ponytail or bun. It falls just past her shoulders and looks like it would feel incredibly soft. She wears simple black pants and a red cashmere sweater. *Cashmere*. Now this version of Vivienne fits the woman I read about online. She looks nothing like the woman I first thought was a biker chick.

"Am I overdressed? Should I wear jeans?"

"No need to change. You look great."

"Thank you. I wasn't sure what to wear for Christmas dinner in a cabin. My family dresses up for Christmas, but I figured fancy clothes don't really go with celebrating the holiday in a mountain cabin." She smiles again. "And look at us, we're Christmas coordinated."

Vivienne gestures to my dark green sweater and then to her red one. Her honeysuckle scent fills my soul and fogs my brain. She smiles with shimmery pink lips. I could take her in my arms right now and make us very late for Christmas dinner. Mom wouldn't even be angry. She was trying to matchmake last night. It doesn't take a rocket scientist to see that's why I'm the person she designated to give Vivienne a ride.

The thought of our conversation last night begins to burn in my gut. Where did these fancy clothes come from? She did not buy cashmere in Davidson. How'd she get it?

"Are you ready?"

"I am. Please give me a moment to collect my coat."

Vivienne disappears into the bedroom for a *moment* and returns wearing a black coat that isn't made of leather but of wool instead. She grabs a wrapped package from the bar and a purse. I don't know purses, but the black leather looks expensive, and I haven't seen her carry a purse before.

"Did you go to Charlottesville shopping or something yesterday? You couldn't have gotten all of this stuff here in town."

"No." She hesitates for a moment and then continues. "Someone from home was kind enough to bring me a few of my things."

Who's *someone*? Is Vivienne being vague on purpose? Is it a boyfriend? Her lady in waiting, whatever that is? I can't ask any of these questions.

We walk together in silence, down the stairs and out to my van. I hold the door open for Vivienne while she climbs inside. Mom would be proud of my chivalrous manners. Of course she drilled them into my head enough.

I get settled into the driver's seat. The silence is starting to get weird, so I say the first thing that comes to mind.

"This van comes in handy for hauling supplies for Mayfair, but I sure miss my Audi coupe."

Vivienne smiles and tucks a stray piece of hair behind her ear. "This is great. Thank you for driving me today. I have been thinking that if I'm going to stay here in town for a while, I should buy some kind of car."

"Do you have a friend who can bring you that, too?" The words are out before I can stop them. I sneak a look at Vivienne in time to see her grimace. "Look, I'm sorry. I don't know why I said that."

"I do."

"You do?" Funny that Vivienne could know why when I have no idea myself.

"Yes."

"Would you care to share?"

"You don't like me very much, do you?"

"Why would you think I don't like you?"

She sighs. "You didn't answer the question."

I think back to what Mom said last night. "I offered you a place to live above my restaurant, and I'm driving you to Christmas dinner with my family. I wouldn't do that for someone I didn't like."

"You did invite me to live at Mayfair, and for that

I'm grateful. But tell me the truth, did you think of driving me to the cabin on your own, or did your mother put you up to this?"

Now it's my turn to sigh. "I get partial credit." Vivienne groans. "I had the thought and was going to ask you myself, but Mom beat me to it." She folds her arms together across her chest. Not good. Not only will Mom be able to tell I've upset Vivienne, I don't want to upset her. I pull to the side of the road and put the car in park. We're on the mountain road now where cars rarely travel.

"Vivienne, I do like you. Why do you think I don't?"

"Because you call me Vivienne. I have asked everyone here to call me Viv, and they do. Why must you insist upon addressing me so formally?"

Really? Someone who says "insist upon addressing me so formally" is concerned that I'm using her full first name?

Vivienne was all smiles when I picked her up. Is all of this attitude because I made that stupid comment about her friend bringing her a car? It was a dumb thing to say for sure but not worth all of this drama.

I tentatively reach across the console and cover her hand with mine. She doesn't pull away. Instead she looks at me with unsure eyes. I do my best to keep my eyes focused on hers, when what I really want to do is look at her hand. Her skin is silky soft beneath mine.

"I like what I know about you very much, but to be honest, I don't feel like I know enough. You literally just kind of slid into my life a couple days ago. You spend your time driving around the country on a motorcycle even though you"—I stop short before saying you're rich. She doesn't know that I know about that. I wish she'd just tell me herself. Instead I catch myself and continue—"wear cashmere. You're like this mysterious puzzle, and I can't make some of the pieces fit."

This is the perfect opportunity for her to tell me about her fortune. I'm not sure how one says to another, *"by the way, I'm loaded,"* but at least if she tells me, I'll know officially. That would take the heat off me, and I might understand Vivienne better, maybe even figure out why she's running around on a motorcycle instead of attending some fancy party in a low-cut gown.

"I'm not mysterious. I can honestly say no one has ever used that word to describe me."

She speaks the words as if she's disappointed. I don't want mysterious. I want simple. I want what-you-see-is-what-you-get. I let go of her hand and bring my fingers to her chin. With a slight nudge, she tilts her head back and looks in my direction. Our eyes connect.

"If I start calling you Viv, will you believe that I like you?"

"It's a start."

"Okay, *Viv,* are you prepared for the craziness of a

Richardson family function?"

She nods. A tiny smile plays on her lips. It's all I can do not to kiss her. Maybe then at least she'd believe me when I tell her I do like her.

I make no move to get closer. Instead, I sit a little straighter and try to return her smile.

Here we go.

Chapter Fourteen

Viv

The drive to the Richardson family cabin takes less than twenty minutes from Mayfair. Once outside of Davidson, Brady turned to the right onto a two-lane road that cuts its way up a small mountain. The road narrows and zig-zigs as we travel higher.

A skilled motorcyclist would love driving on this type of road. I am not that person. While my driving skills have improved since I've been on my little adventure, I still lack the confidence to pull off driving on a road like this.

Brady turns onto a short dirt-and-gravel driveway and parks behind a green Jeep.

"We're here." These are the first words either of

us has said out loud since our *discussion* a few moments ago.

Maybe my reaction to Brady's question was a bit over the top. Well, I know it was. Something about Brady pushes my buttons.

He's right. He did allow me the use of the Mayfair apartment. That was kind of him. Still, the gesture doesn't make up for the fact that he often studies me when he thinks I'm not looking. His eyes take on a steely fire similar to liquid metal. There are looks that we share that betray his nonchalance, like the look he gives me now.

"Stay right there."

Brady exits, walks around the van, and holds the passenger door open for me. He smiles softly, and the gesture brightens his eyes. Much better.

"Did your mother tell you to open the car door for me, too?"

His smile shines. "No, this one is all me. She can't have any of the credit."

Brady pulls two huge shopping bags full of wrapped presents out of the back, and we walk together past several parked cars. How many people are here? Should I have brought more gifts? I carry only one. I had thought one gift for the Richardsons would be enough. But then, I can't be expected to buy gifts for people I don't know.

I study the cabin in front of me. It's clearly large. I believe it's only one story, but there's either a loft in part of it or very high ceilings. It looks real and not at all like the ski cabins we've rented in the past.

I follow Brady up the steps and onto the porch. He slows and then stops walking as he transfers one shopping bag from his right hand to his left, doubling up. Instead of opening the front door, he uses his free hand to gently squeeze my arm.

"I'm glad you're here."

I take a deep breath in and let it out slowly.

The door opens suddenly. Brady jerks his hand away.

"Merry Christmas!" Grace chants. She stands in the doorway wearing a light blue sweater. Elvis's face is sewn into the middle, surrounded by white snowflakes and the words *"My Christmas won't be blue."* The sweater goes perfectly with the King's music cascading out of the cabin.

A dog's bark can be heard over the music. I look down just in time to see a Cocker Spaniel jump up to greet me. He has black fur and wears a green bandana with red and white-striped candy canes.

"This is Winston. He's a sweetie with very bad manners."

I reach down and pet his little head.

"Aren't you a cutie?" I say directly to Winston.

"Brady, do not feed Winston any table scraps. You have him spoiled rotten. Now come on in and say hello."

Grace pulls me in for a hello hug. I can't help but smile. I've never known anyone who has such a fascination with Elvis. Matilda Rollins loved the music of one boy band and then another, but that's when we were teenagers. Grace is easily sixty.

"Get in here, Brady, it's freezing."

Brady steps inside the cabin and closes the door behind him. Suddenly we're surrounded.

"This is for you."

I hand Grace the only gift I have with me. I do have another gift back at the apartment, but it isn't ready yet.

Kate reaches me first. She gives me a tight hug and takes my coat. Hunter's greeting is technically a hug, although much looser than Kate's and ends with a light pat on the shoulder. I receive the same type of greeting from Albert Richardson, Kate's father.

"Hey, I haven't gotten to meet Viv yet."

Albert sidesteps out of the way, revealing an elderly woman with short white hair and a plump stature. She wears a red Christmas sweater with golden jingle bells sewn into the design.

"So nice to meet you, Viv. I've heard a ton about you. I'm Beverly Simms, Hunter's grandma, but you can call me Granny. Everyone does."

An audible jingle emits from her sweater as I'm suddenly embraced by her. My grandmother smells of expensive perfume. Granny smells like sugar cookies with a hint of pine. "I ran into Maybelle at Minnie's yesterday, and she told me you were a cutie pie. Just look at you."

"My turn, Granny." A tall young woman with long

dark hair and emerald green eyes moves from Brady to me. She holds her hand out, and we shake. "I'm Kennedy, Hunter's younger sister. It's nice to meet you."

Once the greetings have finished, I get my first good look at the inside of the cabin. A very large Christmas tree sits in the corner of the room. *Room* is an accurate term for this part of the house; however, the space is quite large, bordered by a huge stone fireplace on one end and the kitchen on the other. It reminds me of the cabin my family rented during a ski trip we took to Colorado one winter. The great room of that cabin was similar in size, but the rental was perfectly decorated to cater to the tastes of the wealthy people who rented it. This cabin is rustic and full of memories and charm. It's perfect.

"You two are just in time for dinner. Brady, you're in charge of drinks for you and Viv. Everyone else, please find your spot at the table and be seated.

I find my place card—a touch I would also find on Grandmother's Christmas table today—between Brady's and Kennedy's. That is the only similarity I have found so far between Christmas at home and Christmas with my lovely new friends.

The table setting is beautiful. Each place has a Christmas plate painted with a decorated tree. A white linen napkin with crocheted trim tied with a bright red ribbon rests on top of each plate. Our table at home is also surrounded by family, only family that doesn't like each other very much.

Brady places a glass of red wine on the table next to my place card before taking his seat at the end of the table. Kennedy sits down as well with a glass of tea. Next to Kennedy is Granny and then Albert at the head of the table. Grace sits next to him, and then Hunter and Kate. It's a cozy group and perfect except for the butterflies that fill my chest. Why am I so nervous?

Albert says the blessing, and then the food is passed. Before I know it, I have a plate full of beef tenderloin, cheesy potato and bacon casserole, and spinach salad.

"This dinner looks amazing. Thank you so much for having me."

"We're happy you're here," Grace says with a huge smile. "It was so kind of you to stay here in town to help Brady and Meg. I'm sure you miss your family today. Your parents must really miss you."

I swallow hard to hold back the instant swell of emotion and clamp down my features. Despite years of Grandmother's etiquette training, I'm not particularly adept at schooling my emotions or my facial expressions. Mom always said it was because my heart was too big to be trapped inside. The thought of Mom only makes it worse. Tears form in my eyes. *Damn*. I don't want to ruin Christmas dinner for these sweet people.

"Oh, dear. What did I say, sweetie? I've clearly upset you."

I take a quick breath and force a smile in Grace's

direction. "I am terribly sorry to let my emotions get the best of me. You see um—thank goodness Grandmother isn't here to hear that *um*—my parents passed away in May. They were in a car accident." Deep breath. "I thought I would be able to handle myself better than this. I truly apologize for my behavior."

"An apology isn't necessary. You poor thing. Do you have any family left?"

I nod. "My grandmother. Grandfather passed away about ten years ago. I also have an uncle, aunt, and two cousins. They all live in and around Boston."

"And your staying here to help us has kept you away from your family." Brady's speaks quietly.

"Yes, however, I think that part is for the best. The more I thought about going home for Christmas, the more I realized how difficult it would be without my parents. I believe it's easier for me to be here."

"We're really glad you're here with us." Kate smiles encouragingly.

"Will you excuse me please? I think I need a moment to freshen up."

Brady scoots his chair back away from the table. "The bathroom is this way. I'll show you."

I follow Brady down a hallway and do my best to keep my emotions in check until I can be alone in the bathroom.

"Viv." The sound of my name makes me pause in the doorway. I turn my body toward Brady's, but I don't dare look him in the eye. I can't. I don't want him to see the tears there. I wish I were better at this. He can tell I'm a mess. "I'm sorry I pressured you to stay here and help us. I feel like a complete ass." He takes a step closer and brings his hand to my chin. He lifts gently until we're eye to eye. "Why didn't you say anything about your parents sooner?"

"I don't know. Dealing with my parents' death isn't the reason I decided to stay in Davidson, but it is a good thing I did."

The Richardsons are such warm and loving people. Their Christmas celebration is full of love, something clearly absent from Christmas dinner at Manningsgate.

A tear falls. Brady dutifully wipes it from my cheek. The sudden realization of his closeness brings my body to full attention. I confronted Brady earlier about not liking me. How are we now in this position? He breaks eye contact as his gaze drops to my lips. His own lips are only inches from mine. Is he thinking about kissing me? My body warms at the thought. I could initiate the kiss. It would be easy to do. In a matter of inches, our lips would be touching.

Brady takes a step back. Too late. The moment is over. Brady's face flushes like only a redhead's can.

"I'll see you back at the table. Take your time."

Then he's gone.

Chapter Fifteen

Brady

"Is Viv okay?" Kennedy asks, but it's easy to see the question on the faces of everyone at the table.

"I think so. She just needs a minute."

"Why are you so red-faced?"

Crap.

Why am I so easy to read? It was all I could do not to pull Vivienne to me and kiss her until she was happy again. She looked so vulnerable. Heat flashes again. Can they tell?

"Aren't you a little young for hot flashes?" Granny asks with a chuckle. "I had them something fierce when I went through the change."

I open my mouth to correct her, but it isn't

necessary. The smirk Granny wears clearly shows she's teasing me. I'm really not in the mood. Granny knows no boundaries. Hunter deals with this kind of thing on a regular basis. I usually laugh from the sidelines. I'm not laughing now.

"Did you kiss her?" *Kate.* Of course. We aren't twins, and yet she's somehow always too in touch with my emotions. "Oh, you didn't kiss her. You should have, you moron."

I flash a look to Mom before she gets in on this. She closes her mouth. Thank goodness. There's no telling what she was about to add to the conversation.

"Not that this is any of your business, but Viv is my employee. There will be nothing going on between us. Get it?" I look from Mom to Kate and then Granny. "Got it?" I give Kennedy a glare as well, just for good measure. She folds her lips inward to keep from laughing. My family is so freaking annoying sometimes. Kate married Hunter, and somehow all of Hunter's family is now mine. Even his crazy Granny. Is it supposed to work this way?

Viv rounds the corner, and all eyes are on her. While her cheeks still appear to be pink, she's generally brighter. She takes her seat again between Kennedy and me.

"Let's start over," Mom announces. "Viv, we're very glad you could spend Christmas with us. Kennedy honey, why don't you fill us in on what you plan to take next semester." Mom turns her gaze to

Viv. "Kennedy's a junior at Virginia Tech. She's majoring in Mechanical Engineering, and she's really something."

Viv smiles a smile full of relief as Kennedy launches into a list of classes that sound impossibly technical.

✣✣✣

"Where did you find this?" Mom stares open-mouthed at the present she just opened. It's the gift from Viv. Mom turns it so we can all see the painting of the Richardson General Store.

"I painted it yesterday afternoon."

"You are incredibly talented." She is. The painting depicts what the front of the general store looks like—the brickwork, the cobalt blue front door, and the glass display window. Whether it's the lighting or some other artist's tool, the painting captures the feeling of the general store as well. "Did you know Viv could paint?"

Mom looks at me. I had no idea Viv could paint. Add that to the list of things I don't know about her.

"I knew." A sudden flare of heartburn works its way up my throat at Kate's glee in harboring intel about something the rest of us didn't know. I swallow hard. "Viv bought some painting supplies at the store the other day." Kate speaks the words directly to me. She knows I'm bothered, but why do I care? A big sigh escapes, and I shake my head.

Maybe my in-tune sister will tell me that, too.

She stands and looks around the room. "Is everyone finished opening their gifts?" The sounds of rustling paper subside as we all now look at Kate. She looks as if she's about to burst with excitement. Hunter entwines his fingers with Kate's. He smiles and doesn't take his eyes off my sister. "We just wanted to let everyone know that we're going to have a girl."

Maybe the cancer drugs have given Mom super speed because she reaches Kate with a hug before anyone else. Granny pushes in behind Mom. The rest of us wait our turn to congratulate the couple. Hunter beams with excitement.

"Can I help you repaint my old bedroom for the baby?" Kennedy asks. "The room needs a fresh coat of paint for sure, but I guess that means painting over the Eiffel Tower as well. That would be too bad."

"When Justin and I painted your room that awful color, we obviously had no idea what we were doing." Hunter wraps his arm around Kennedy. "It was a little too pink, don't you think?"

Kennedy smiles. "Maybe, but I never minded. The gesture was so thoughtful I didn't care. Not only did you paint it my favorite color, you took the time to paint the Eiffel Tower on my wall, too."

Kennedy's being polite. Granted, Hunter and his brother, Justin, were practically kids themselves, but the Pepto pink they chose to paint Kennedy's bedroom walls was not right. I've slept in that room before. It's like the pink is electric.

"You won't be upset if we repaint it? Say a lighter shade of pink?"

"Of course not. I'd say that's a good idea."

"Good, because we already did. We painted it about a month ago."

"Did you know the gender of the baby then?" Mom asks this one.

"No," Kate answers with a chuckle. "I just had a feeling and went with it. It was sad painting over the Eiffel Tower. Maybe I can buy a stencil or something. A Parisian theme would be really cute for a nursery."

"Can I paint it?" All eyes move to Viv. She blushes slightly, yet somehow I feel the warmth. "I'd love to paint a mural for your nursery, and I have some free time while I'm here."

"Seriously? That would be fantastic." Kate pulls Viv in for another quick hug. "You have to let us pay you, though."

Viv stands a bit straighter. "I most definitely do not want payment. If you buy the supplies, I would love to do it. In fact, Mayfair is closed tomorrow. If it's okay with you, I could get started then."

"Thank you."

I can feel Kate's excitement from here, but it probably isn't my almost twin-powers this time. Everyone in the room can likely tell her feelings at this moment.

My sister is having a baby. Sometimes the

thought just hits me hard. It's a lot of emotion to take and too much when I'm in front of so many people. I need a diversion.

"Who's ready for dessert?"

"What do you think?" Granny asks as I take my first bite of her coconut cake.

The morsel scrapes across my tongue like sand from the Sahara. I take another look at what's left of the piece on my plate. How does it look so good and taste so bad? Granny waits expectantly for my response. I take another bite to buy myself some time. This one isn't any better. The frosting and pieces of coconut stick to the roof of my mouth. You'd think at least the frosting would provide more lubrication than it does.

I take a sip of my coffee and glance at Hunter, whose mouth is spread in a wide grin. His piece of cake remains untouched. Granny's bad cooking is legendary, but with Meg's help, she's improved lately. Her chocolate cake recipe is delicious. We just had it at Thanksgiving. So what happened to this one? I swallow hard, and the cake goes down.

"It's pretty good. I think I just really like the chocolate cake you make more. It's hard to compare the two."

Granny looks at me suspiciously and takes a bite herself. She quickly frowns. "This sucks."

I open my mouth to contradict her and then close it. She's right. It does suck.

"Did Meg teach you how to make this cake?"

Granny shakes her head. "No. Frank's daughter gave me the recipe. She said Frank likes this one, so I thought I'd learn to make something other than chocolate cake. I followed the recipe exactly. I don't know what could have happened."

"When is Frank coming home?" Kate places her hand on Granny's shoulder.

"Late tomorrow afternoon. I guess it's good I have another day to practice."

"Maybe Meg has some time to go over it with you in the morning before Frank arrives."

"Sorry I experimented for our Christmas dessert. I think I got a little over-confident about my baking abilities, and now we have nothing for dessert."

"We have plenty of sweets lying around." Mom gets up from the table and returns with a platter of homemade cookies and a huge box of chocolates. She gives me a wink. Of course. Leave it to Mom to have a back-up plan. I shouldn't be surprised. Granny grabs a chocolate chip cookie and munches away.

"Since I'm sad about messing up dessert,"—she doesn't look that sad honestly—"I get to pick teams for Trivial Pursuit. It's me, Brady, Kate, and Albert against Hunter, Viv, Kennedy, and Grace."

Viv's gaze meets mine, and we share a quick smile. I hope she can handle what's about to happen.

This game can get a little heated. Last year was the first time Granny was with us for Christmas. That didn't stop her from getting into an argument with Dad about the Jackson Five and which of the members had solo careers.

Kennedy gets the game board set up as we rearrange ourselves at the table. Viv sits right across from me and next to Kennedy.

"You're going down," Viv says with a twinkle in her eye. Okay. So maybe she'll be able to handle herself after all.

Several questions in, and it's clear that my team is at a serious disadvantage. Hunter knows a little about a lot of things, Kennedy knows all the science questions, Mom seems to know all there is to know about entertainment, and Vivienne seems to know everything about everything. She knew the name of Claude Monet's house in France and the name of Vincent van Gogh's roommate. Who knows this stuff?

"How did you know that?"

"I spent a little time in Provence with my family. We visited the city of Arles on that trip, where van Gogh lived with Gauguin."

Vivienne pronounces Arles with an accent that sounds like she's actually French. Kennedy practically swoons.

"I've wanted to go to Paris my entire life. Hence my obsession with the Eiffel Tower. You've seen it?"

Viv nods. "I have. I'm sure you will make it there

someday."

"I have a Paris-fund going. There isn't much money in it, but I'm working on it. Someday I'll get to go."

"No doubt about that."

Viv and Kennedy share another smile. What is there to smile about? Why would a person who summers in Provence travel to Davidson on a motorcycle? Does it have something to do with her parents passing away? Did their passing make her penniless or even more loaded?

The fact that I know so little about Vivienne burns in my stomach. I could do more research on Viv if I wanted to. There was plenty of info on the web about her. *No.* I can't do that. I feel guilty enough for what I found out the first time I looked.

It's so frustrating that the only real thing I know about Viv I read online. Why do I even care? You'd think I'd be smarter than this after all I've been through. You'd think my whole family would be smarter than this. Instead, we're clearly all sucked in by Vivienne's charms.

"It's getting late, Mom. I think we're going to go."

I expect Mom to protest. It's only eight thirty. When she doesn't, I take a good look at her. Dark circles have formed beneath her eyes along with a heaviness to her lids. She pushes herself up from the table, catches me watching her, and then transforms herself with a smile. My eyes meet Kate's. She saw it, too.

Mom insisted we celebrate Christmas together here at the cabin. We should have protested more. Of course it was more work to have our dinner here than at their home. Dad and I brought the Christmas tree here and helped Mom decorate it. That's all Mom would let us do, but we should have pushed harder to help.

A sensible person would have used paper plates. Not my mother. She lugged her Christmas dishes, all the food, and presents. I'm sure she did a thorough cleaning of the cabin as well. Next time we won't take *no* for an answer.

Chapter Sixteen

Viv

Brady's been quiet for too long. I know he's worried about his mother. I finally take the plunge and ask him about it.

"What kind of cancer does your mother have?"

Brady sighs heavily. "Ovarian. They operated last month. The doctor thinks they removed it all, but he did some chemo to be on the safe side. Those treatments just ended, and Mom's worn out from the whole ordeal."

"She's a very strong woman."

"Yes, she is. She's also very stubborn, which is why I think she insisted on having a huge family Christmas at the cabin. She wanted to prove to herself and to all of us that the cancer didn't beat her."

This isn't witty banter, but at least Brady's talking. He carries the shopping bag containing the gifts I received—a travel easel from Kate and Hunter, a sweater from the Richardsons, and a hand-crocheted scarf, hat, and mittens from Brady himself. I take the bag from Brady so he has two hands to unlock the back door at Mayfair.

"Your family is so thoughtful. I can't believe you all purchased gifts for me. I was happy to be invited to join you for Christmas dinner. That gesture itself was more than enough."

Brady holds the door open. I enter the small hallway, and Brady follows.

"What do you do for a living?"

My eyes gulp for air and then my lungs. I turn and face him.

"Why do you ask?"

"You're a contradiction, and I want to make sense of you. Do you have a job?"

"Not exactly."

His lips form a thin line.

"There you go. Another vague answer." He sighs. "You did go to college, yes?"

"Yes."

"Where did you go? What did you study?"

"I went to Columbia and majored in art history."

Brady's body relaxes some. "That explains how you knew some of the answers to the Art and

Literature questions. Most people avoid the purple category when they play Trivial Pursuit."

"How can you afford to travel around the country without a job?"

I shrug. "I have some money saved up." That isn't a lie exactly.

"Okay. How about this? You're well-educated and without any visible tattoos, so why are you traveling around the county on a motorcycle? You don't exactly look the part."

"It's kind of a long story."

Brady smiles. "I have the time."

My turn to sigh. "I haven't always had the best luck in my life." Brady nods for me to continue. I haven't shared the truth with anyone. I'm going to tell Brady—I owe him that much—but it seems odd having this conversation in this darkened hallway.

I set the shopping bag on the floor and lean back against the wall for support. I take a deep breath and tell him.

"My grandmother calls the shots in my family, and I have done what she expected of me for my entire life. I went to the schools she chose for me, I associated with the people she wanted me to know, and I participated in the activities she deemed appropriate. The only time I ever pushed back was with my degree. My grandmother thought political science or pre-law would be better choices. I finally convinced her the degree I received didn't matter. I went to Columbia, a university she approved of.

Finally, she gave in and let me study art history."

"Your parents just went along with whatever your grandmother said?"

"Yes. Everyone goes along with whatever my grandmother says."

Please don't ask why. I don't want to tell Brady about the money, but I don't think I can *not* tell him if he asks me a direct question. He doesn't. Brady adjusts his weight to his opposite foot and looks at me, waiting for me to continue.

"Other than my choice of majors, I have done everything I was told to do and created a life for myself that was exactly as my family expected. None of it made me happy. The only happiness I've ever had was when I snuck away to paint."

Poor little rich girl.

That's what I sound like to myself. It's pretty ridiculous really, whining that my life is so horrible when there are people in this world with much bigger problems. Brady's eyes are soft and show his concern.

"So you left?"

I shrug. "After my parents' accident, I decided to take some time to figure out my life. Right around that time, I was stuck at a red light that just happened to be next to a Harley Davidson dealership. I found myself daydreaming about what it would be like to ride a motorcycle. I imagined a carefree life and surmised it was fate, so I went with it. It was a gorgeous day and perfect riding weather.

"I pulled into the parking lot, marched right in, and bought what they had available. I didn't even have a license. The owner gave me private lessons and helped me get my license.

"Owning a motorcycle was the farthest thing from what was expected of me, and that fact made it feel right. I decided to trust fate to decide what I should do next. I had no plans. I just rode every day and stopped when I needed to stop."

Brady's forehead creases. "What did your family think of that?"

"Grandmother was furious when she discovered what I'd done. Riding a motorcycle was not on her approved list of activities. But my parents had just passed away, so she finally relented and gave me some space. Maybe she saw my determination. I don't know. I just knew I had to get away. This was my one chance to figure out what I wanted to do with my life. I still don't know what I want, but I do know I want more than that life."

"Did you find what you were looking for?"

"Truthfully, my trip was pretty awful until I came here. I rode down the eastern seaboard to Miami and then started back up north. I have seen a lot, but the trip hasn't been the spectacular adventure I was hoping for. Well, until I came here to Davidson. One minute I was cursing myself for riding in the rain, and the next, I met you and soon had a job. It was surreal but also the first real thing to happen to me since I left home in June. The people here are so genuine, and no one wants anything from me."

"You said something like that the other night. Is this usually a problem? What do people want from you?"

Too much. I quickly close my mouth and bite the inside of my cheek. I've said enough for one night.

"It doesn't matter."

"It matters to me. I can't fall for another pretty woman with too many secrets."

The air in the small hallway seems to hum with energy. I swallow.

"You think I'm pretty?"

Brady brings his hands up level with my head and braces them against the wall behind me. His eyes darken and somehow show both confusion and determination at the same time. I look into them as long as I can before my gaze is drawn to his mouth as it moves closer. He touches his lips lightly to mine and stills. Just this slight contact sends a shiver through me. My lips part with a quick intake of breath, and it becomes much more than a convergence of lips. It becomes a touch of our tongues and then even more as his body presses me against the wall.

Brady breaks our kiss.

Too soon. I'm not finished yet.

My arms move around him to pull him even closer, and our kiss begins again. Heat flashes between us.

Is this what I've been hoping for? What I get for

trusting fate? *This is a kiss.* It isn't two people trying to make a connection when there's nothing drawing them together. It's two bodies connected by more than just a bringing together of skin. It's passion, and it's what I've been missing in my life and why I went on this ridiculous journey in the first place.

Brady steps back, breaking contact altogether. "I shouldn't have let that happen."

I smile despite the unsure look on Brady's face. That was the most amazing and real kiss I've ever experienced in my life. He was kissing me for me. He wasn't doing it to get in good with my family. He knows nothing about my family. The thought brings an even bigger smile. I won't let Brady run away from me. I take his hand.

"Come with me."

He plants his feet. "I don't think that's a good idea."

My smile grows. "Not for that. I have something for you."

Brady lets me lead him up the stairs. I open the door easily. There's no point in locking it. It's Christmas Day, Mayfair is closed, and I have nothing of value here anyway except for my antique compact, and that's only of sentimental value.

I set the bag of gifts down by the door, flip on the light switch, and close the door behind us. Only then do I release Brady's hand. An open door is not a good idea right now since it feels like he might flee at any moment.

"Wait here. I'll be right back."

I find the painting exactly where I left it on my dresser. It was still wet this morning, so I knew I couldn't wrap it and bring it along with us to the cabin. I hold it facing me and carry it out to the living area. Brady stands near the door in exactly the same position I left him.

"This is my Christmas gift to you."

I turn the painting of Mayfair around so he can see it.

I study his reaction. His mouth opens, but words don't make their way out. Brady takes the painting from me and steps closer to the bar. He holds the painting under the light there for at least a minute before he finally lifts his head and looks at me.

"You painted this? You're really good."

"Thank you. I didn't bring it earlier because it had to dry a little longer." And it felt awkward to give it to Brady in front of his family. It's just a painting, but somehow I wanted to keep it just between us. I want to keep the reason between us, too.

"It doesn't even compare with the gift I gave you. Thank you."

"You are welcome. Would you like a glass of wine? In addition to clothes, my friend also included a couple bottles of Opus One. Want to share one with me?" Brady glances at his watch and shifts his weight from foot to foot as if he's suddenly standing on hot sand. "It's just a glass of wine."

"It's not just a glass of wine. A bottle of Opus

goes for at least two hundred, and that's for a recent vintage."

"It was bottled last year. Don't get too excited."

"It's still a lot of money for a bottle of wine to drink on a whim."

"This isn't a whim. It's Christmas."

"Okay." Brady doesn't look convinced. "I'll go downstairs and get some glasses and a corkscrew."

He turns and walks out the door. I say a quick prayer to myself that he'll return, and he does. Brady opens the wine and pours it into a decanter to breathe. He then takes the decanter in his hand and swirls it around to aerate it even more. Finally, he pours each of us a glass. I take my glass and walk over to the small couch in the living area.

Brady follows. He sits down next to me and sets his wine glass on the coffee table. He rubs his hands on his knees and then picks them up and places them in his lap, clearly uncomfortable. I take a long sip of wine to buy myself a little more time. Brady stares at something across the room.

"She messed you up pretty good, didn't she?"

"Who?"

"The woman who made it impossible for you to trust other women?"

"It's not quite that bad." Brady's deep exhale lets me know her betrayal has had more of an effect on him than he'd like to admit, possibly even to himself. "You probably know all about Jamie. Everyone in this town is a gossip, and my family is right there in the middle of them all."

"Your family cares about you deeply."

"True, but they still talk too much. They don't understand what it was like to be so blindsided. They trust everyone they meet. Geez, they took you in practically off the street and trusted you immediately. Mom thinks she's this great judge of character and would know if someone was trying to pull something with her. Well, I'm no idiot, and I had zero idea Jamie was using me in her diamond smuggling operation. I mean, *diamond smuggling*. Who would ever think something like that is going to touch their lives? Pardon me if my experience made it difficult for me to trust people."

"You can trust me, you know."

Brady grunts and stands up. I think he's headed for the door, but he stops after only two steps and turns back towards me.

"How can you say I can trust you? I realize I've only known you a few days, but you're clearly keeping things from me and everyone else. What do you have to hide?" Brady's pale blue eyes are radiating.

I stand and step towards him, lightly touching his arm.

"I admit I'm keeping things from you, but they aren't bad things."

Brady executes an eye roll. I can't blame him for being impatient. I want to tell him everything. I can't. People always change once they find out who I am. Once I consider someone a friend, it's never the same. I want to see where this goes first. If the kiss we shared downstairs is any indication of what's to come, I can't let Brady know about the money. I don't want Brady's feelings for me to change, just like everyone else's always does.

"If these things aren't so bad, then why hide them?"

"I have my reasons. You have to trust me."

"I can't do that right now."

Brady turns and walks out the door without looking back.

"Merry Christmas, Rose."

"Merry Christmas, sweetie."

"Sorry to be calling so late, but I know you had church this morning, and I haven't had a chance to call until now."

And I just really needed to hear a friendly voice.

"What's he like?"

"Who?"

"The man you're with. I overheard Rebecca speaking with your grandmother yesterday. Is he who you were with today?"

Great. I had briefly forgotten about my babysitter. How much did he see today? He couldn't have seen the kiss in the darkened Mayfair hallway.

The kiss.

Tears threaten, but I shove them away. There's nothing to cry about. Brady and I shared an amazing kiss. I know Brady felt the heat of that moment just as much as I did. It was a lot to process, especially for someone who has trust issues. I understand how he feels since I rarely trust anyone myself. It's just that, with Brady, it feels different. Most people are trying to worm their way into my life. Brady keeps trying to push me away, which seems to make me like him even more. Maybe this is some kind of reverse-psychology thing.

"Viv, sweetheart, is everything okay? Would you like me to come down there?"

A tear escapes from the corner of my eye and slides down my cheek. "No, that isn't necessary. What I would really like, however, is for you to retire."

"What?"

"I apologize. I shouldn't have been so blunt with my words. What I mean is that I think you've spent enough of your life working for our family. I know you have enough money saved up to retire and move to Florida like you've always wanted. I am the reason you're still working, aren't I?" The silence from the other end of the phone makes it clear my theory is correct. "I would like to give you a retirement bonus to make it easier for you to retire now."

Hey, if I'm going to have to take on the role of being a Prescott, I might as well spend my money on what I want to spend it on.

Rose stammers but quickly regains her voice. "Viv, while I very much appreciate what you're doing for me, I can't let you go through with it. I will retire when I'm ready."

"That is exactly why I want you to retire now. I'm thirty years old. I need to be able to stand on my own two feet without the Prescott fortune. I need to figure out a way to be on my own, and I can't continue to hold you back while I figure it out. Rose, I love you. Will you at least consider my proposal?"

"Only because you want me to." Rose's voice catches. She's crying now, which gives my own tears the permission they were seeking to fill my eyes and practically waterfall down my cheeks. "We can talk about it when you come back home."

Home. That gigantic house my family has called its own for generations seems less and less like home by the day.

Chapter Seventeen

Brady

"You painted all that in one day?"

Viv jumps about two feet off the ground and lets out a squeak of surprise. One hand flies to her chest as her face flushes a darker pink than the pale shade that now covers the walls of the nursery.

"Brady!" She takes a quick breath and releases it. "You shouldn't sneak up on people like that."

A chuckle escapes me. I quickly bite my upper lip to keep it inside as Viv is not amused.

"I didn't mean to scare you. I swear. I knocked on the front door before I opened it, and I called to you from the living room. I think your music drowned me out. Besides, Kate told me you were expecting me."

Viv pants a couple more times as if I caught her aerobicizing in here instead of painting the baby's room. Her color returns to normal, and I get my first good look at her.

Adorable.

She probably wouldn't like that description, since that's not what women usually go for, but she is what she is. Viv's honey-brown hair is pulled back into a ponytail. A few pieces of hair have escaped and hang freely near her cheeks. She has a smudge of gray paint on her right cheek. Like I said—adorable.

The room is suddenly filled with energy and warmth. I think Viv feels it, too, because she looks away. She takes her phone out of her pocket, pushes a button, and the heavy rock and roll stops abruptly.

"I guess I was just caught up in my work."

I close my fists, shove my hands into my coat pockets, and rock back and forth on my heels as I examine her painting. An Eiffel Tower spans the distance from the floor to the ceiling. Much of the detail is penciled in and still awaiting the stroke of Viv's paintbrush, but the outline is done. It's quite striking. A gray life-sized poodle has been painted at the base of the tower. It's cartoonish enough to fit in with a nursery but still filled with the details that only an experienced artist can pull off.

"You are really talented. Do you sell a lot of your work?"

Viv's blush returns. "No. I've never sold a painting."

"You could, you know."

"Thanks. I've never tried. Painting has always been a hobby, something I use as an escape."

An escape from what?

I close my mouth hard to avoid asking the question out loud. Sure, I'm dying to know, but at the same time, I don't need to go down that road again. It's clear Viv doesn't want to talk about certain things. I have to respect that. She'll tell me what she wants me to know when she wants me to know it.

"Well, if you ever need a quick way to make money, you have it. You're really talented."

"Thanks." The corners of Viv's mouth lift up to form a small smile. "Give me just a moment to clean up my mess, and I'll be ready to go."

"Take your time."

She doesn't. The painting supplies are quickly collected and stacked in the corner of the room. "Let me just clean these brushes." Viv walks to the kitchen. I don't follow. Instead I walk out onto the front porch and sit in one of the rocking chairs.

My own little home doesn't have a front porch or a view of a pasture. Instead, I have a small deck at the back of my house that overlooks a small back yard and the tiny deck of Phil and Miriam, my neighbors who live behind me. It's fine since I'm never out there anyway. Of course, if I had a porch like this, I might spend more time outside.

Viv opens and closes the front door. "Should I lock it? Kate said she won't be home for a few more hours."

"I'll do it."

I separate the house key from the others on my keychain, insert it into the lock, and turn. It doesn't pass my notice that Hunter and Kate trusted Viv to be in their home all day without them here. Of course, I trust her to stay in the apartment above my restaurant. That has to count for something.

I turn away from the door and stop short so as not to run into Viv. Her closeness was unexpected, and I have nowhere to go without making it awkward. She looks away, a move that only increases my uneasiness.

We stand together like this for several long seconds until Viv finally speaks. "Listen. I want to ask you something." She again makes eye contact. Her soft blue eyes uncertain.

"Okay."

Viv bites her lip as if she's deciding if she should actually ask me a question.

"I know I stayed in town to help you out at Mayfair and all, but if you want me to go, I can leave."

What?

My stomach seems to drop out of my body, leaving me with a sense of almost panic. Viv feels suddenly too far away. I resist the urge to pull her to me. Instead, I reach out and lightly squeeze her forearm.

"Why would I want you to go?" Viv shrugs her shoulder and looks away. "This is my fault, isn't it? I overreacted about what happened between us last night. I'm the idiot who's being too cautious with you. It's obvious I like you, but I'm also afraid of you." Viv's gaze returns to mine. Her forehead wrinkles in a slight frown. "You've said yourself you can't tell me everything, and I know you'll be leaving town after the holidays."

Her eyes glisten. Her mouth opens with a quiet sigh. My restraint disappears. I bring my lips to hers, and Viv reacts immediately, parting her lips even more to allow my tongue entrance to explore her mouth. A feeling spreads through me, half tingling and half numbness. Two opposite feelings that somehow work together to spread warmth through me and urge me onward.

Is this what Viv wants?

The thought barely registers before she tucks her hands inside my coat, grazes my sides, and then pulls me even closer. My hands move through her hair to her neck and down her back, which I can hardly feel beneath her coat.

We have *way* too many clothes on.

The thought jolts me back to reality. I pull away. Viv licks her swollen lips and smiles at me. She places her hands firmly on my hips.

"I guess if I don't want anything to happen between us, then I should probably stop kissing you, huh?"

Viv smiles. It isn't a big smile with lots of teeth. It's more of a brightening of her eyes. Eyes that seem somehow wholly innocent, although they're connected to the hands that rest on my hips. Viv's said what she's hiding isn't bad. Can I believe her? I really want to believe her.

"Would you like to go to dinner with me?" The invitation pops out somehow before it even formed as a thought. I'd only been enlisted to give Viv a ride home—not that I hadn't thought about having dinner with her. Once the words are spoken, I can't take them back. I don't want to take them back. Maybe if we spend some time together, just the two of us, I'll learn more about her. Maybe if we spend some time together, she'll tell me.

"I would love to have dinner with you, but first I have to change my clothes."

"Actually, where we're going, you're dressed just fine."

Chapter Eighteen

Viv

Brady's resolve to stay away from me is softening. At least, I hope so. There's no denying he feels something for me. Last night I lay awake thinking maybe I'd imagined Brady shared my feelings the first time he kissed me. But now, after he kissed me again, I know Brady feels this pull between us just as much as I do.

I gave Brady an out when I asked him if he wanted me to leave. If he wanted me to go, then he could have said yes. He didn't. Instead, he kissed me. A kiss like we shared means something. I hope it means more than lust. The lust is present for sure.

I thought Brady was attractive when I first met

him. The attraction I feel for him has only gotten stronger since that moment. It hasn't even been quite a week yet, and I can't stop thinking about him. In fact, since I spent almost the whole day today painting in the nursery, I had too much time to think about Brady, Grandmother, Henry, and the guy following me. All of it played through my thoughts in a constant loop.

Painting is usually cathartic for me. It helps me work through my problems. I figured out today that the first issue I have to solve is how Brady feels about me. I had to know why Brady walked out on me last night. Is it because he likes me and is afraid to get close to me, or is it that he just plain doesn't want to be around me? There could be other reasons, but those are the ones that seemed most likely. My thoughts were less dramatic than the whole *If-you-love-someone-let-them-be-free* thing but still along those same lines.

Brady has certainly become an issue in that I cannot stop thinking about him. He's such a good man. Given his past luck with women, it's no wonder he's gun-shy about having a relationship. It might be different if I could stay here in Davidson indefinitely. That can't happen. As nice as it is to have this little interlude, I have to go home and take my place in the family. That's what Grandmother has always expected of me. No one tells Grandmother *no*.

But I did.

I told Grandmother I was staying in Davidson for

the holidays, and I did it. The world didn't end. But that was only for a couple weeks. Is there any way I can say no to Grandmother for good and stay in Davidson as long as I want? She would never go for that.

The small parking lot adjacent to Minnie's Diner appears to be full. Brady drives past and takes the next available angled parking space on the street. I exit Brady's van and breathe in the chilly nighttime air. The moon has risen enough so I can see it above the roof of the diner ahead. We walk in mostly-comfortable silence.

It isn't that it feels awkward, necessarily. It's more that I want to know what Brady's thinking.

Is this a date?

He did ask me to dinner after kissing the snot out of me. That kind of makes this a date, right?

Brady holds the diner door open for me. I feel a blast of heat as we walk inside Minnie's Diner. The oldies music playing is difficult to hear over the noise of people talking. The place is packed. We stand near the door, trying to take it all in. Every booth is full, and there appears to be only one stool available at the counter.

Kennedy walks over to greet us. She carries a coffee pot in one hand and wears the Minnie's waitress uniform of a button-up pink cotton dress. Her long, dark hair is back in a ponytail and tied with a scarf. She gives each of us a quick hello hug with her free hand while holding the hot coffee out to the side.

"It's pretty crazy here tonight. There might be a bit of a wait for a table, but I'll keep my eyes out for you."

"They don't need to wait. They can share with us." Granny Simms joins our group. "Frank just got back from visiting his daughter, Carol, in Germany."

Granny grabs my hand and pulls me with her as she turns and heads down the aisle. I make eye contact with Brady. He gives his head a small shake and follows us. There's clearly no arguing with her anyway. Granny stops at a booth where a nicely dressed older gentleman sits. His silver-white hair is combed over to attempt to hide his obviously bald head. He smiles at us with kind, pale blue eyes.

"Vivienne Prescott, this is my boyfriend, Frank Baker. Frank, this is Viv. She's the one I told you about who's in town for a couple weeks to help out at Mayfair."

She gives me a wink before sliding into the booth next to Frank.

"It's very nice to meet you, Vivienne. Good to see you, Brady."

I sit across from the elderly couple. Brady sits next to me although not as close as Granny and Frank sit together. I'm not sure they could sit any closer. The plates in front of them have some remnants of food, although I cannot make out what they had for dinner. I can tell there was mashed potatoes and gravy. That's all that looks familiar.

Frank whispers something in Granny's ear. Her response is a deep, throaty laugh.

I brave a glance at Brady. He rolls his eyes dramatically.

This. Is. Strange.

Kennedy comes up and takes our drink order. "Granny, would you and Frank like dessert tonight? There's chocolate cake."

Granny doesn't take her eyes off of Frank. "We're going to have dessert at home tonight."

"Okay."

"Then we're going to have the coconut cake Meg helped me bake today."

I can't help but chuckle, more out of shock than anything else. Granny turns and looks at me as I feel the blush take over my face and neck.

"I apologize for my outburst. I am truly sorry."

Granny's smile is huge. "Don't worry about it, dear. Older people are just like everyone else. Frank's been away for two weeks, and I've missed him, if you know what I mean."

"We *all* know what you mean, Granny." Kennedy rolls her eyes.

"Someday, God willing, you'll be old. Trust me. You'll be happy someone invented Viagra." Granny smiles triumphantly. "Come on, Frank, let's blow this popsicle stand." She scoots out of the booth. Frank follows and plops two twenties on the table. Kennedy picks them up.

"I'll get your change."

"You keep the change. Nice to meet you, Vivienne."

Kennedy holds the bills out towards them, but it's too late. They're gone. For an older couple, they move fast.

"Sorry about Granny." Kennedy sighs. "I don't know what to do with her sometimes."

"Granny has been without Frank for two weeks. Of course they want some alone time together." Brady raises his eyebrows.

"I get it," Kennedy agrees with a wistful sigh. "I haven't seen William for two weeks, and I won't get to see him for another two."

"Hey there everybody."

A young policeman walks up to the table and stands next to Kennedy. He's tall with dark hair and light grayish-blue eyes.

"I have to check on my tables." Kennedy nods at the young man and then rushes away, leaving the policeman to stand awkwardly next to our table.

"Viv, this is Bryce Chambers. He works with Hunter."

Sitting in this booth makes it impossible to stand, but I extend my hand for a handshake.

"Crazy crowded in here tonight, huh?"

"Yeah. Would you like to join us?"

"Nah. Thanks for the offer though. I'm going to sit up at the counter." I look up to see that a couple more spots have opened up. "I just came by to say hello. Nice to meet you, Viv. I'll see you around."

I watch as Bryce takes a seat on the stool at the end of the bar.

"Did he and Kennedy have a bad break-up or something?"

Brady shakes his head. "He and Kennedy never dated. Besides, Kennedy was just pining over the guy she met at college, William."

"True. It just seemed like there was some kind of energy between Kennedy and Bryce. You don't think so?"

Kennedy returns, ending the conversation. "What can I get you to eat? It's Monday. You know what that means?"

I look back at her, and she smiles. "Okay. Maybe *you* don't know what day Monday is. It's meatloaf day."

I return her smile as confidently as I can. "Do you like meatloaf?"

Do I? No idea. While this adventure has opened me up to many new dishes, such as biscuits and gravy, I have not experienced meatloaf. However, I cannot let Brady know that.

"Of course." I answer as confidently as I can. "Everyone likes meatloaf."

Brady visibly relaxes back into the cushioned seat of the booth. What was that? Some kind of test?

Kennedy begins clearing away the dirty dishes left by Granny and Frank. "I'll have your dinner right out."

She gives me a quick smile and rushes away. The

spot across from us that's now void of dirty dishes seems oddly vacuous. Brady and I sat together on this side of the booth because the other side was taken by Granny and Frank. Now, it seems a bit intimate over here. I like it, but I don't know if Brady feels the same way. I wait in silence a few beats to see if he moves or mentions moving to the other side of the booth. Luckily, he doesn't even inch away from me.

"What was it like to grow up here?"

"Same as anywhere else, I guess."

"I don't think so. Davidson is special. The people here really care about each other."

"I think that's a nice way of saying the people here are nosey."

"No, I'm serious. Maybe the people talk a bit more than they should, but they do that everywhere. Here, at least there are genuine feelings behind it. It's not just a bunch of gossiping. People aren't only out to get what they can from each other."

"You've mentioned that before. Do you always think people are out to get you?"

"Not so much out to get me. They aren't trying to bring me down. They just usually want to use me to their advantage."

"What do you have that they want?"

Money. My connection to the power of my family. I don't say either one. I can't let Brady know about that yet. Although I'm ninety-nine percent sure that it's me he likes and not the money, I can't be sure. He has to tell me himself. Of course, people have lied to me before. In that regard, I know Brady won't let me down. He is not a liar.

"It doesn't matter what it is. People are generally trying to get something from every relationship."

"Do you still *only* want to work at Mayfair? Is that all you want from me?"

Good question. I decide to go for the honest approach.

"I want you to like me for me."

"Okay. Who are you? It's hard to like you for you if I don't know who you are."

"Fair point. You know all of the important things. I like to paint."

"Have you ever smuggled diamonds?"

"No."

"Have you ever smuggled anything else?"

"I took my own candy into the movies once, but I felt so guilty about it, I left it in my purse and bought some in the lobby anyway."

Brady's expression becomes flat. "Are you on the run?"

"What?"

"I'm serious. It can happen, you know, even to normal people. Are you in danger? Is that why you're hiding who you are?"

"No, it's nothing like that. I've told you who I am. I even gave you a copy of my driver's license." How can I tell Brady the truth without actually telling him? "It isn't anything so dramatic. I am not happy in the life that I have. I think I'm meant to live a different life. That's all."

"What kind of different life? Are you married?"

"No."

"Engaged?"

"No."

Sort of. This conversation is moving into dangerous territory. There has been no question asked or ring exchanged. It's more of an agreement between our families. That isn't technically an engagement, it's serfdom. Besides, the one thing I have decided on this trip is that I'm not going to marry Henry. I don't love him, and I refuse to spend the rest of my life with him.

Kennedy plops our dinner down in front of us. I guess you would call these *plates* of meatloaf, but their size and oval shape make them look much more like platters than plates. There is certainly enough food on them to feed more than two people, and yet we each have our own.

"Here you go. Enjoy." Kennedy bounds off and leaves us alone again.

"Wow. This is a lot of food." It really is. A huge slab of meatloaf takes up a third of the plate. Another third is mashed potatoes covered with gravy, and the last third is split between corn and green beans. "You definitely get your money's worth here. Can you imagine serving such huge portions at Mayfair?"

"No, I cannot." Brady smiles and takes a huge bite

of the meatloaf. "This is one of the best dishes they have. That's probably why it's so crowded in here tonight. People don't want to waste Meatloaf Monday on left-over Christmas turkey or ham. That'll be around for days."

I follow Brady's lead but with smaller amounts of food. I stab a piece of meatloaf with my fork and then drag it through the potatoes and gravy. I taste all of it once and see right away why Meatloaf Monday is so popular. Grandmother would likely die if she saw me right now. The thought makes me smile.

"What is it?" Brady asks.

The truth is so many things. I love meatloaf. Who knew? I love trying new things, especially when I like them so much. I like it that Brady continued to sit next to me after Granny and Frank left for dessert. I can't tell Brady any of those things. Instead, I keep it simple. "This is just really good meatloaf."

He returns my smile and goes in for another bite.

The front door opens, and I catch a glance of Gerard as he walks inside.

Great. Has Gerard already made his report to Grandmother? *Your granddaughter just kissed the snot out of some man. Would you like to see a photo?*

Gerard smirks and gives me a nod. I try to hold onto my smile for Brady's benefit, but I feel it slip. He stops chewing and looks up at the door.

Oh no.

Gerard turns his head away from me and heads down the row of barstools before Brady looks up. He chooses a seat next to Bryce, the policeman I just met.

Why does he still have to be here?

"Do you know him?"

"No." Technically not a lie, but I feel the sting of it anyway.

"Are you okay?"

I sit up a little taller so as to project my most confident self. "Yes. I haven't eaten anything since early this morning. I'm just hungry."

I'm pretty sure Brady doesn't believe me.

Chapter Nineteen

Brady

My past dating experience has left me completely paranoid. How could Viv know this man? She knows no one in Davidson. Viv hasn't looked in his direction since he walked in. So the guy caught her eye when he came through the door. I've watched several people come and go since we sat down. I'm being ridiculous.

It's definitely not a surprise that the man's eyes might stay on Viv a little longer than necessary. She's gorgeous. I sneak another look in his direction, catch him watching us, and give him my best *She's-with-me* look. He shrugs and turns to speak with Melinda, who's just walked up to take his order.

It's not really fair for me to get all territorial over Viv. I've given her plenty of reasons why anything between us won't work. At the moment, however, I can't remember any of them.

I take out my phone and send Bryce a quick text.

The guy sitting next to you. Any idea who he is?

I continue to eat my dinner nonchalantly as I watch Bryce pick his phone up from the counter and read my text. Our eyes lock for a split second, and then he types his reply.

Never seen him. Is there a reason I should keep an eye on him?

I know the answer right away. I can't ask the Davidson police force to harass every man who gives Viv a second look. That's way over the top ridiculous.

Not necessary. Just wondering.

I focus my attention back on Viv, who has put a bigger dent in her meatloaf than I'd have thought she could manage. She must have been starving. It never occurred to me to make sure she had lunch today. I'm sure Kate remembered—Kate never forgets those kinds of details—and probably left food for Viv. I'll take Viv lunch tomorrow and make sure she actually eats it.

"Dessert?"

Viv's response is a laugh and a big inhale and exhale. "There is no room for dessert after that huge meal. It was delicious though. What's the special tomorrow?"

"Fried chicken. It's heavenly."

"How do you people not weigh five hundred pounds? I feel like I have gained ten since I arrived."

"No idea, but it isn't because of our good eating habits."

I leave enough money on the table to pay the bill and still have enough left over for Kennedy to have a healthy tip. I help Viv slide into her winter coat. I don't know fabrics and brands and all that stuff, but I do know Viv's coat was expensive. The wool is softer than any winter coat I've felt before.

It doesn't take a leap of imagination to see that Viv's wealthy. She spends time in France, and she has two hundred dollar bottles of wine lying around. The fact that she's never had a waitress job, yet she knows the little things to do and when to serve the bread and butter.

Why does she insist on keeping her money from me? Does Viv think she can't trust me?

We both hug Kennedy goodbye before stepping back outside into the cold. I purposefully avoid looking at Bryce when we leave just in case he's checking out the guy next to him. I don't want him to know we're in cahoots. Maybe he'll learn something about our mystery man.

"Can I walk you home, or would you rather we drive?"

Viv smiles and takes a deep inhale of the cold air. "I'd rather walk if that's okay."

"Walking is perfect."

The moon is higher now and beautiful against the dark sky. The temperature has dropped considerably in the short time we were inside Minnie's. Viv's cheeks are already taking on a rosy glow. Her ponytail bobs up and down as we walk. As nice as it felt to run my hands through that long soft hair, what would it feel like to have it out of the way, allowing full access to her neck. My body warms despite the cool temperature.

Snap out of it.

I've been lucky to spend some time with Viv over the last couple of days, but tomorrow will be different.

We turn into the alley and arrive at the back door of Mayfair without saying a word the entire way. I unlock the door, and Viv steps inside. I don't follow.

She stops after a couple steps, turns, and walks back to me where I still hold the door wide open.

"You're not coming in?"

"I don't think that would be a good idea."

"Why not?"

"Mayfair is open tomorrow, and you're still my employee."

"Temporary employee. I won't be in town for

much longer. I don't want to waste the short amount of time I have with you."

I appreciate Viv's honestly, but the reiteration that she'll only be here a short amount of time is part of the problem. I don't have time to get to know Viv as much as I need to know her to allow anything to happen between us. I have to protect myself.

"I'm the one with the issues, you know."

Viv leans in and kisses me lightly on the cheek.

"Goodnight, Brady. Thank you for dinner."

Viv lets herself inside. Without a word, I walk away because I am the biggest dumbass in the world.

❖❖❖

This nagging restlessness has been with me all day. My brain keeps demanding that my body stay away from Viv, and I have. I didn't bring her lunch. I didn't pull her into my arms for a kiss when I arrived at Kate's to pick her up for work. Even after watching her work to put the finishing touches on my future niece's mural. Even when she turned and smiled at me, and I got a view of her paint-smudged nose, I stood my ground.

I've done nothing but think about this woman all day. If it wasn't enough that Viv's loaded and completely out of my league on so many levels, or that she hasn't told me about the money, her time here in Davidson is about half over. What's the point of starting something with a woman whom I know is going to bail? I can't do that to myself.

Now we're alone in my van, and my memory of the reasons why I should stay away from Viv is fading with every honeysuckle-laced breath I take. We sit in awkward silence as I try to think of something to say. I already told Viv her mural is amazing. That was easy to do because her work is incredible.

Viv's version of the Eiffel Tower is almost as intricate as the real thing, not that I've seen the real one in person, but I have a good imagination. It's painted in a dark charcoal and highlighted with varying shades of gray that are picked up in the poodle and the Arc de Triomphe. It's fantastic work.

"I can't believe you painted all of that in only two days."

"Me either. I haven't painted since my parents passed away. Since I've been here, it's like the painting is springing from inside me, trying to get out or something. This has never happened to me before."

Viv's watching me. I can feel her gaze on me without taking my eyes off the road ahead. I don't respond to her words. I have no idea what to say. Instead, I try to look like I don't feel the meaning of the words she just spoke in my gut. Is she really insinuating I'm responsible for this change in her painting habits?

I don't say another word for the few minutes

remaining in our drive. I pull into my usual spot in the alley behind Mayfair and exit the van before the moment turns intimate. My resolve is slipping. I need to get away from Viv before I do anything stupid.

She doesn't wait for me to open her door. She rounds the front of my van, stops short, and folds her hands over her chest.

I'm in trouble.

Viv stares at me as if waiting for me to speak. I don't dare say a word. I have a sister, and I've seen this seething look before. Sooner or later, she'll tell me what I've done wrong.

"What exactly is going on with you?"

"What are you talking about?"

Viv stands straighter, emitting a heavy sigh. "I'm talking about how you treat me. Do you really only want to kiss me on your days off?"

Now it's my turn to sigh.

"I told you that I don't approve of relationships at work. Besides what they can do for morale, I'm your boss."

"Your reasoning is ridiculous. I'm only working for you temporarily." Viv's right. I don't dare open my mouth to answer. I shrug instead. "I just can't believe that's what you want from me."

"What?"

"You want me as an employee instead of... anything else?"

The loud chirp of my phone makes me jump.

Although I wouldn't normally answer a phone call in the middle of a conversation, it seems like my savior right now. *Saved by the bell* and all that. I muster an apologetic look and answer the call.

"Brady, it's Dad."

His words are full of worry.

"What's wrong? Is Mom okay?"

"I'm not super concerned, but I want to let you know. Your mom has a slight fever. We're at the emergency room as a precaution."

Viv squeezes my arm. There's no anger left in her eyes, only compassion.

"I'll be there as soon as I can."

But how can I go? I'm needed here at Mayfair. We open in an hour.

"You go." Viv's words are soft. "We can take care of things here. You need to be with your mom."

"She's in the ER."

"I heard your father."

"But I can't leave."

"Look at me." I raise my head and look into her brown eyes, the color of soft caramel. "Do you trust me?"

"Yes."

I answer without even thinking. I do trust Viv.

The corners of her mouth tip upward in a small smile. "Go to your mom and dad. We've got this. I know how much Mayfair means to you. We won't let you down."

"I'll be back as soon as I can."

I kiss Viv quickly on the cheek and hop back into my van, praying that both Mom and Mayfair will be okay tonight.

Chapter Twenty

Viv

"Rebecca, I beg of you. Would you please ask Grandmother to call this goon off? Gerard is everywhere, and I do not need a babysitter."

Gerard walked by the alleyway after I watched Brady drive away. Brady had to see him.

"Mrs. Prescott heard about your kiss last night. After that, I don't think she'll be discontinuing Gerard's services any time soon. She's very upset and concerned Henry might find out."

I want to scream, *"Who cares about Henry?"* from the rooftops. I bite my tongue and say nothing. While I've decided I will not marry Henry, arguing with Rebecca about him will accomplish nothing.

"Is Grandmother available? I'd like to speak with her."

"She is not. She's at the club with Mr. and Mrs. Prescott."

Right. It's Tuesday, Uncle Patrick and Aunt Vanessa's standard date with Grandmother for drinks and dinner. I swallow my frustration. Maybe Uncle Patrick will put in a good word for me. I'm not sure why he's so interested in my well-being, but if he's on my side about me staying in Virginia for a little longer, I'll take it.

"Would you please speak with Grandmother and try to persuade her? I promised Grandmother that I will be home after the holidays, and I would really like to have some time alone with my new friends. They are good people. I'm safe here."

And Gerard is going to mess up everything.

"I will pass on the message, Ms. Vivienne."

That's all I can ask for, I suppose.

"Thank you, Rebecca. Goodbye."

I disconnect the call and make it down to the kitchen just in time for the staff meeting.

"Did you have a good Christmas?" Meg asks as she pulls me in for a hello hug. "Kate sent me a photo of what you painted in the nursery yesterday. She can't wait to see how it looks today."

"I hope it's what she was looking for. I'm happy with how it turned out, and it was really fun to paint."

Meg smiles. "I think it's much more than what

she was expecting. I can't wait to see it."

"I have to tell you something important. Have you spoken with Brady recently?"

"No. Where is he?"

"He got a call a few minutes ago. Grace is in the emergency room. She has a fever."

"That can be serious when you're having chemo treatments, but I'm not sure about afterwards. She had her last treatment a couple weeks ago."

"Albert said he was taking her to the hospital as a precaution. Our Christmas celebration was amazing. Perhaps Grace overdid her efforts there and is simply worn out. Either way, I insisted Brady go to the hospital to be with his family. He's been worried about his mother, and I knew he had to go."

"The fact that Brady actually went to the hospital tells me how worried he is."

"I know I just started working here, but I can do anything you'd like me to in order to fill the gaps."

We walk together to the empty space designated for our meeting and stand together in our small circle, which feels even smaller without Brady.

"Let's get started," Meg begins. "We have a lot to talk about today. First, some good news. Rhonda is recovering nicely. I ran into her husband, Mike, at the general store this morning, and he gave me the good news. She was able to come home from the hospital on Christmas Eve. So far, so good with her recovery."

"That's great," Katherine remarks. "What's going

on with Brady? Did you say he's at the hospital?"

Meg's smile falls. "His mother was taken to the E.R. a little while ago. Grace isn't feeling well and has a fever. You know how devoted Brady was during her cancer treatments. I'm sure he's a nervous wreck."

"Is there anything we can do for him?" Leo asks.

"Yes. We need a plan for how we can run this place tonight without Brady. I won't be of much help out there in the dining room since I can hardly ever make it out of the kitchen. What do you think, Katherine? What's the best way to handle the staff we have?"

"Viv should take Brady's place at the front."

"What? You and Manny can't manage waiting on all those tables by yourselves."

"I'm sure there will be times when the service we provide isn't as impeccable as it should be, but I think this plan is much better than having no one up front to greet our guests at the door. You are the most well-spoken of all of us, and you know the most about wine. You could be our greeter and the sommelier for the evening. If you have any time in between, you could help with tasks like filling water glasses and clearing the dishes. My thought is that if we greet our guests warmly, then maybe they will forgive us if we have a serving slip-up here and there."

"I like it," Meg announces.

"What do you think, Leo?"

He shrugs. "I don't have a better idea."

"We'll share our tips with you. That way you'll still make as much as you would any other night."

Leo grimaces at Katherine's words but doesn't disagree verbally.

"I very much appreciate the gesture, but it isn't necessary. You deserve whatever tips you get tonight."

"You at least get the tips for whatever wine you sell. That only makes sense."

"I insist you keep all the tips. Brady and I will work something out later."

Meg smiles and then looks up at the ceiling. That is not what I meant, but any back-peddling I do now will only make me sound more guilty. While I definitely wish I was sleeping with my boss, I am, unfortunately, not.

✣✣✣

All in all, the plan is working pretty smoothly, despite the times when we get slammed—look at me using restaurant terms like I've worked here for years. The thought brings a smile to my lips.

I do realize I might be working myself out of a job, but I try not to think about that. This work is temporary anyway. The fact that I'm proving Mayfair can be run without me isn't the smartest thing I've ever done, but I'm doing it for a good reason. Mayfair is important to Brady, and Brady has become very important to me.

At least the good part about the busy times is that I have less time to worry about Grace. The woman has been so sweet to me since I've been here. I wish I was there with Brady and his family. The thought makes me sigh to myself. I'm not a part of his family, but they've been nicer to me than my own. I've grown to care for them so much in the week I've been here in Davidson.

Brady especially.

If I hadn't already decided not to marry Henry, spending time here would have helped me make the same decision.

Henry has kissed me on two occasions. Once when we were in college and the arrangement between our families was formally discussed. We'd had the kind of long dinner together that stretches for hours. It was almost midnight when we were saying goodbye, and he leaned in and kissed me. I hated it. If it wasn't bad enough that the kiss was emotionless, the audacity of it made my blood boil.

Henry leaned in without warning or hesitation. His tongue demanded entry to my mouth, which I firmly denied. I was livid. He laughed. *"You'll open everything when we're married."*

I still can't believe he was so brash. Henry came back the next day and apologized, blaming the hours of cocktails and wine for his actions. Grandmother thought he was sincere in his apologies. She said I should give Henry another chance. My own parents agreed with her, because in my family, Grandmother gets what she wants.

So I let Henry grovel for as long as I thought I could get away with and then forgave him—at least, I told him that I forgave him. I did mean to, but it's clear now that I haven't made much progress in that endeavor.

Henry's a jerk who's used to getting what he wants. A man like Henry can never be faithful to one woman, especially a woman he's only marrying for family connections.

Our second and last kiss wasn't as bad, but it certainly didn't leave me wanting more. He kissed me when I left to come on this trip and told me that it was good for me to get my wandering out of my system before mothering his children. That moment pretty much sealed his fate with me, but since Grandmother agreed with Henry on that point, I didn't make my arguments then and there.

Brady is nothing like Henry. Brady is kind, he works hard, and he cares about others. He's close with his parents and sister. He's a good family man. And when he kisses me, it's like the world is on fire. My face flushes at the thought. I've never had it this bad for anyone.

Chapter Twenty-One

Brady

Being here in this hospital is so draining. It isn't just the stress of tonight. It brings back all the emotions I've felt since we found out Mom had cancer back in October. Bad news of that nature can really throw a person for a loop. Even though Dr. Hanover gave Mom a good prognosis from the beginning, it was still ovarian cancer. Too many mothers, sisters, and daughters die from it each year.

The last couple of months have been a constant reminder that death can take us at any time. Look at the accident last week. What if Mom hadn't been able to stop her car in time? What if Viv had been seriously injured from her slide on the pavement?

I might never have known her. I might never have known the tingle of her touch or the heat of her kiss. She's been the subject of almost every thought I've had, whether waking or dreaming, since I met her. What did I even think about before last week?

Mayfair, mostly, I guess. I should be more worried about Mayfair tonight and how things are going without me. Instead, my thoughts are mostly devoted to Mom and Viv and the determination in her eyes that told me in no uncertain terms that I was coming to the hospital tonight. She promised that she and the others would take care of my restaurant, and I believed her.

They did, too. I don't have a full report, but Meg texted me three times to let me know all was going well. She could be lying just so I won't be concerned, but I don't think she is. Meg owns half of Mayfair and worries about the place just as much as I do. If she says the evening is under control, then it is.

"They're going to move your mom to a regular room, so she can stay here for the night. The doctors just want to keep an eye on her. They've given her some medicine to help her sleep. I'm going to stay here with her, so why don't you all call it a night?" Dad looks exhausted. I think about suggesting he go home for a little while to get some sleep, but I don't bother. There's no way Dad's going anywhere.

Kate stands and stretches her arms over her head. "Hunter and I will stop by the house and get Winston. We can dog-sit for as long as you'd like us to. Is there anything else we can do, Dad?"

"Not for now. You get some rest too, pumpkin. You're sleeping for two."

We say our goodbyes to Dad, who walks back into the emergency room to be with Mom. Kate, Hunter, and I walk together to the parking lot.

"I knew Mom overdid it with the Christmas festivities. I wish she would have let us help her." Kate's eyes moisten. She sniffs and then takes a deep breath. I know exactly how she feels. Not just because of our sort of twin-powers, but also because I feel exactly the same way.

"I should have pushed her more to let us help. I believed Mom when she said she had everything under control. I shouldn't have listened to her. Mom and Dad are both getting older. They can't do everything they used to do. Look how tired Dad looks."

"They have to realize they have limitations," Hunter adds. "Neither of them are bound to do that anytime soon. They're both as stubborn as mules."

Kate wraps her arms around me for a goodbye hug. I'm not sure if it's my imagination or not, but I'd swear she can't get as close as she usually does with her baby bump in the way.

"Don't stay up too late tonight," Kate whispers as I let go.

"What do you mean?"

"You know exactly what I mean," she says with a smirk.

Stupid twin-powers.

⁂

I pull into my usual spot behind Mayfair. My headlights illuminate Meg as she walks out the back door.

"Did everything really go as well here as you led me to believe?"

"It really did. There were a few small issues that we remedied with free desserts. I promise you that everyone left here happy. How's your mom? Is everything okay?"

"She will be. As we guessed, she overdid it with her Christmas preparations. I'm glad this setback wasn't caused by something more serious. She should be okay after getting some rest."

"Did they admit her to the hospital?"

"They did but hopefully just overnight. No one can get rest in that place."

"You need to go up and tell Viv. She's been worried sick."

"Thanks for holding down the fort tonight. I'm really thankful I could be at the hospital with my family."

"Everyone pitched in. Now stop stalling and go see her." Meg's smile is somehow crooked and caring at the same time.

Am I that transparent to everyone? At this point, I don't even care. I just want to see Viv.

"Goodnight, Meg."

"Goodnight," she replies in a sing-songy know-it-all kind of voice. It's no wonder Meg's such good friends with Kate.

I don't give Meg another thought. It's Viv I want to see. I take a quick peek in the kitchen to make sure it's dark, and everyone else has gone home. They have, so I head up the stairs toward Viv's apartment.

Viv's apartment.

She hasn't even lived here a week, and yet it feels more hers than mine. I give my head a shake and knock lightly on the door. She probably isn't asleep yet, but just in case, I don't want to wake her up. Viv opens the door wearing jeans and a sweater under her long winter coat. She holds the hat, scarf, and mittens I gave her for Christmas in her hand.

Where could she be going this time of night? It's after midnight.

"Going somewhere?"

She smiles. "I was worried, and I knew there was no way I'd be sleeping. So I thought I'd go down to the hospital to check on your mom."

"How were you going to get there?"

She stands a bit straighter, as if preparing for a fight. "I was planning to walk. It's only a couple miles, and it isn't too cold out. How is she?"

"She's good. Just really tired. They gave her something to help her sleep and are keeping her overnight for observation."

Viv's smile grows. "That's a relief."

"You were really going to walk all the way to the hospital in the middle of the night?"

"Yes. I was worried about you all."

"Can I come in?"

Viv jumps to the side to allow me entry. "Of course. Please do."

I step inside. Viv slides out of her coat as do I. She takes them both and lays them across one of the counter stools.

"Can I get you anything? Maybe some wine or some water? Or, I could make a pot of coffee."

"I don't want anything to drink."

Viv's eyes warm. Her smile grows.

Chapter Twenty-Two

Viv

Brady's lips crash onto mine. His kiss is demanding, but nothing like Henry's first kiss that only wanted to take control. Brady is all in, and so am I. I open my mouth to him and immediately feel the heat of his tongue inside my mouth. A whimper escapes from my throat.

Finally.

It's not just that finally Brady is letting go and really kissing me. It's so much more than that. *Finally* I'm being kissed by a man who only wants me for me. I can feel the difference. His arms move around my waist and then down over my backside. He pulls me even closer.

In response, I run my hands through his hair and down the back of his neck.

I need more.

I slide my hands down Brady's back to his waist. I tug at the hem of his shirt and untuck it from his pants. I begin working on his buttons one by one. I want to leave him with no question about what I want. If my movements aren't enough to let him know, then my kiss says the rest. I can be demanding too, and I give this moment everything I have.

Brady pulls away long enough to unbutton his cuffs. I slide his shirt down his arms. It falls to the floor. He moves to kiss me again, and I press my hands against his chest to stop him.

"Not yet," I whisper as I pull his white t-shirt up over his head, revealing his hard chest. I knew from our previous encounters it would be nice, but I'm not prepared for how lovely his chest actually is. The muscles are defined from his pecks all the way down to whatever the muscles are called that slip under his waistband.

I swallow hard as I force my eyes back up to meet Brady's.

"My turn."

He pinches the waistband of my sweater and gently tugs it up and over my head. I feel my body flush and say a silent thank you to Rose for packing this lacy black bra. It's so much nicer than the cotton models I wore while on the road.

Brady's smile stretches from ear to ear. He

lowers his head and kisses each breast through the fabric. I concentrate on standing since it suddenly isn't very easy to stay upright. No matter. Brady reaches down behind my knees and scoops me up into his arms.

My eyes widen in surprise as I wrap my arms around Brady's neck. He smiles and kisses me again as he carries me into the bedroom and places me gently back on the floor next to the bed. Once I have my footing, I begin working on the button of his dress slacks. He kicks off his shoes and steps out of his pants.

He's a boxers guy.

I take a moment to appreciate his body. I have had limited experience in viewing the almost-naked bodies of the men I have slept with. There have only been two, and neither was nearly as well-endowed as Brady in every aspect.

Brady wastes no time in removing my jeans, leaving me in only the black lace bra and panties. My body flushes again. How do I compare to other women he's been with? The prickly heat of embarrassment travels up my chest and neck to my cheeks.

Brady brings his fingers to my chin and tilts it upward. Our eyes meet. "You are so beautiful, Vivienne Prescott. I don't want to waste another second of our time together. I want to be with you for as long as we can be together."

"Really?"

"Really. And let me be clear about what I want from you, because I want a lot."

"Okay." His eyes darken even more. "Tell me."

"I want you. All of you. I want to make love with you tonight and every chance I get."

Our discussion is over. I pull Brady to me. His kiss is softer than before but still more full of passion and meaning than it seems possible for one kiss to convey. Brady's kisses travel down my neck to my shoulder.

He moves my bra strap to the side and plants a kiss on that spot. Fire shoots from my shoulder to my middle. He smiles against my skin and continues his exploration along my collarbone and down my chest to the tops of my breast, where he plants small kisses. He runs his tongue over my nipple. Even through my bra, I'm left panting for more.

He reaches behind me and unclasps my bra. He slowly frees each arm and cups my breasts in his hands. My body shudders. It's been a long time since I've been with a man. I don't know how much more of this I can take.

My hands move to his waist. I slide them downward slowly over Brady's hips, taking his boxers down with them.

Brady's naked.

This is really going to happen. For once, I don't have to worry about someone wanting to sleep with me for money or power or any other reason. Brady doesn't even know about my money. He's here for *me.*

I lean backwards and allow myself to fall onto the mattress. Brady watches me for a moment and then crawls onto the bed beside me. He places his hand flat on my stomach. My hips arch upward. His hand slides downward and then inside my panties.

A whimper escapes as I arch into him again. A few deft movements from Brady, and I'm already so close. I can't wait any longer.

"Brady, please."

He slides my panties down and moves on top of me. I feel him there, poised and ready. I lift my hips to meet him, and he slides into me effortlessly.

"Oh." I think the word and feel it and shout it as Brady moves inside me. Again and again. He calls my name as we come together in a moment I can only call ecstasy.

We lay together, side by side, in silence as our breathing returns to normal. My thoughts alternate between the fact that I just had the most mind-blowing experience I've ever had and that I'll have to leave Davidson soon.

When exactly?

I didn't give Grandmother a specific date. I told her I would be home after the holidays. Rhonda just came home from the hospital a couple days ago. Surely she won't be able to return to work for a couple more weeks, right? Waiting tables isn't a desk job. There's a lot of moving around and heavy lifting. She'll need to be completely recovered to be able to perform the required tasks.

"That's not a happy face. What are you thinking about?" Brady leans up on his elbow and looks down at me. He frowns slightly. "Tell me the truth."

Can I? Will he think me clingy for wanting to stay in Davidson as long as possible and maybe forever, or will he be happy I want to stay? Either way, I do have to tell Brady the truth.

"I was just pondering when Rhonda will come back to work."

"In a hurry to get away already?"

"Not at all." A smile plays on his lips. He's teasing me. "It's the opposite, actually. I really enjoy being with you—not just in bed. Since I'm supposed to go home when Rhonda comes back to work, I was just thinking about how long it will be before she returns. Do you have any idea?"

"I'm not sure. Her family hasn't given me a definitive timeline. I don't think they know." Brady caresses my cheek. "We have two servers on vacation who will be back after New Year's. You won't have to work as often once they return. Having them back from vacation will make things easier on everyone."

"Oh."

I guess Brady thinks me too clingy. I prattle on about how much I like him, and he mentions that he won't need me in a couple days. My eyes moisten with tears.

"Wait. That's not right at all. Let me finish." He

sighs. "I only meant that you've been working so hard since you got here. You've done so much to help me, and I don't want you to have to work so hard. I also don't want you to leave. I want you to stay here as long as you can."

"Really?"

"Absolutely. What just happened between us may be the best moment of my life so far. We've only known each other a week, and I feel like I've been waiting for you my whole life."

"I know exactly what you mean."

Chapter Twenty-Three

Brady

So much for not falling too fast. Viv has me head over heels and spouting romantic words in a week. I knew the moment she took her helmet off in the rain that I was in trouble. I just had no idea then exactly how much trouble.

The sun peeks over the horizon and shines brightly through the window. I need to speak with Kate about curtains or shades or something. Now that Christmas is over, maybe Kate will be able to spend more than a couple hours spiffing this place up. I want the apartment to be a nice place for Viv to stay.

We fell asleep in the wee hours. Our time

together could only be described as *magical*. Geez. If Hunter or Bryce could hear my thoughts, I'd be screwed. Viv makes me have all these romantic thoughts, not fit for a manly man. I don't care.

Can I help it that I'm sensitive and women think I'm a nice guy? It's been a blessing and a curse my whole life. Is that what drew Viv to me? Whatever made her like me, I'm glad she does. She's amazing, and she's in my bed. Well, I guess it's her bed, but technically it's mine. It's the bed we shared last night.

I roll out of that very bed, slip on my boxers and t-shirt, and head to the kitchen area to get some coffee brewing. Maybe tonight we can stay at my house? Is that jumping the gun? Viv and I both agreed we want to spend as much time together as we can before she has to leave. We'd be more comfortable at my place than here.

There were no phone calls during the night—a fantastic thing when your mother is in the hospital. More than that, there were no interruptions in my time with Viv. The thought of it has me springing to life again.

Geez, I can't slow down to save my life. I've tried to keep my distance from Viv. I've tried to keep our relationship friendly and professional. It was a losing battle from the beginning. Last night, despite the fact that I sat in the hospital with my family, worrying about my sick mother, I couldn't get Viv out of my head.

I kept replaying our earlier discussion over and over again. My conclusions were that I should stop being so afraid of what could happen between us and let myself go.

I've held myself back from women for more than a year. Viv didn't orchestrate that motorcycle slide to meet me. It was an accident. She literally slid into my life that morning. Viv trusted fate to take her to the next place, and I realized I needed to do the same.

The doctors ran a few quick tests and gave Mom something to calm her early on in the visit. Most of the evening consisted of us taking turns checking on her and watching her sleep. Mom's fever was gone after a couple hours of treatment.

Admittedly, I was afraid to leave the hospital and go back to Mayfair. I still wanted to be there for every doctor update. Hunter and Kate stayed put as well.

Learning Mom had cancer was a shock to our whole family that we're clearly not over yet. Mom's weaker than she was before the cancer, which is why we all should have told her to slow down.

When I first arrived at the apartment last night and saw Viv wearing her coat, I wasn't sure what to think. Where on earth could she have been going at midnight? When she'd told me she was planning to walk to the hospital, all my composure was gone. The thin walls I'd built inside me to keep her away from my heart began to crumble. One more kiss, and they were destroyed.

It doesn't matter that Viv hasn't told me about her wealth. She'll tell me when she's ready or maybe not at all. What does it really matter? I can't think of a nefarious reason she'd keep it from me. I'm sure she has her reasons. She keeps talking about what people want from her. It's likely she's trying to make sure I'm not another one of those people who want her for the wrong reasons.

I want her for her.

The ring of Viv's phone cuts through the silent morning. The name *Rose* flashes on the screen. I pick it up off the bar and walk towards the bedroom. Viv meets me in the doorway, wearing a sleepy smile and a nightshirt.

"Here you go."

I hand her the phone and turn back to the kitchen to see about the coffee. Viv returns to the bedroom, speaking into her telephone in hushed tones.

Who's Rose? A friend? Is Rose the person Viv said knows her the best? The person who has Viv's phone number for an emergency call?

Is this call an emergency call?

Thank the Lord the coffee is done brewing. I pour coffee into two cups, saying a silent thank you to Mom for giving Viv these cups to use in the first place. Bringing Viv a cup of coffee would be a nice gesture from a nice guy, right? And not at all like a stalker who wants to know what the hell she's talking about in there. *Right.*

I walk slowly towards the bedroom. The distance is only about fifteen feet from the kitchen to the bedroom door. I walk slowly so as not to spill the hot coffee. It has nothing to do with being sneaky.

"Do you think she plans to do anything about it? I can't have her showing up here. She'll mess up everything."

Viv looks up as soon as I walk through the door. She sits on the edge of the bed. I smile and raise the cup with a bit of flare so she knows why I'm here. I place it on the nightstand and retreat. I've already heard enough of her conversation to make me feel like a complete stalker and to keep me thinking and wondering for days.

Who is *she?* A family member? Maybe her Grandmother? If so, what will be messed up if *she* shows up here? *Here,* as in Davidson?

I take a long sip of coffee and will myself to stop thinking about Viv being up to something. I'm just paranoid because of all I've been through in the past. I can't allow these nagging thoughts to screw up what little time we have together.

"That was Rose. She's a family friend."

I turn around to see Viv walking towards me, phone in one hand and mug in the other. This is a good sign. She's volunteering information without me asking. She places her phone on the coffee table and continues into the little kitchen.

"Is everything okay?"

"I think so. She overheard part of a conversation my Grandmother had with someone else. She wanted to talk with me to see what I could make out from the bits of conversation she heard."

"Did you come to any conclusions?"

"No, but I did caution her that it isn't sensible to make assumptions when you don't have all the information. Don't you think?"

Message received loud and clear. Viv's talking about me right now and the part of her conversation I overheard. I think she is anyway. But then, I'm not a rocket scientist, and I feel like she's telling me the truth.

Thinking is overrated, and I've done enough of it in the last twenty-four hours to fry my brain. Instead, I pull Viv to me tightly and run my hands down her back to her waist. It feels good just to hold her like this. I lean down and place a kiss on the top of her head.

"I need to run by the hospital to check on Mom. Would you like to come with me? We can get some breakfast on the way."

Chapter Twenty-Four

Viv

The sun shines brightly, but the temperature has really dropped since yesterday. I wonder how much it snows here in Virginia. I haven't seen any snow yet this season. Usually, at home, we've had a couple good storms by now.

Brady holds my hand as we walk to Leslie's, the gourmet bakery where Kate bought that amazing pear tart the other day. I'm so hungry right now, I think I could easily consume four of those delicious pastries in one sitting.

Brady's gesture is a sign that we aren't hiding whatever is happening between us. He also invited me to come with him to visit Grace in the hospital. I like having our relationship out in the open. We might as well. Grandmother knows Brady spent the night with me last night.

I almost panicked when I saw Rose's name on my phone, thinking it was Grandmother calling again. The last thing I need is to have Grandmother scolding me with Brady in the room. She's likely to call soon though. The fact that she hasn't called me yet only makes me think she will come here to Davidson herself. She already sent Rebecca here to retrieve me without success. Making a visit herself is her logical next move.

If Grandmother does visit in an effort to make me come back home with her, will I be able to tell her no? I don't want to go home.

Thank you, Rose, for giving me some warning. I need to strengthen my reserve. I promised Grandmother I would return to Manningsgate after the holidays. I need all the time I can get to figure out a way to stay in Davidson longer. This place feels more like home than Manningsgate ever did. How can I possibly make Grandmother understand that?

Will she insist *after the holidays* means January second? When I made that promise, I meant I would go home when Rhonda returns and Brady and Meg no longer need me to work at Mayfair. Brady mentioned last night that the vacationing servers will return soon. A normal person would be able to bide their time and stay here as long as they want. With the kind of intelligence Grandmother is getting from Gerard, she will know the missing Mayfair staff has returned before I do.

How did she know about Brady staying over? Doesn't this man sleep at all? He can't watch me all the time. Brady's van being parked outside the restaurant all night likely gave away our tryst.

If Gerard would just mind his own business.

If Grandmother would simply trust me. I've never given her any trouble at all, well, only once when I decided to buy a motorcycle and go on an adventure. It seemed like a good idea at the time.

It *was* a good idea all around. I trusted fate to show me a different life, and fate has done just that. Fate brought me here to this little Virginia town where magical things have happened. I have a job and, dare I say, a boyfriend.

I'm smiling to myself as Brady opens the door for me to enter. The scent of sweet, succulent treats fills the air. I breathe in deeply, and my mouth waters as I take in the long glass case before me.

We take our place in line, and I size up my options. The pear tarts are available, but they also have a banana nut muffin that catches my eye. It's unfair to give something so decadent such a simple name. The lemon loaf also looks phenomenal. Maybe I really will have to order four items just to try them all.

"I'm going order the sausage, egg, and cheese breakfast sandwich, well maybe two of them. I'm absolutely ravenous." Brady brings my hand to his lips and kisses my palm. "They have some other heartier choices as well if you're not in the mood for something sweet."

I study the breakfast menu. There are only a few choices, but one of them is ham and brie on a baguette. That is exactly what I have for breakfast almost every morning when we summer in Provence. This past summer was the first one in my life that I didn't spend in France. The trip didn't feel right so soon after Mom and Dad's passing, and then there was my impromptu motorcycle adventure.

Seeing the choice somehow feels like Mom is smiling down on me from Heaven. That's exactly what I'm going to order.

We order our breakfast and two coffees and sit together at a table in the corner. The space is small, with only a handful of bistro tables. Most of the patrons get their orders to go.

The little bell above the door announces the arrival of another person. I look up in time to see Gerard enter. I don't bother to school my distasteful expression. In fact, I glare in his direction. He lifts his shoulders as if it's some type of apologetic gesture. What message is he trying to get across? *"Sorry I told your family you slept with your boss."* Well, no thank you. Apology not accepted.

My look must be scary enough to send him running because he turns around and walks back out the door. Good riddance.

"What was that about? Isn't that the guy from the

other night at Minnie's?"

Oops. I wasn't thinking of Brady when I glared at Gerard. The satisfaction of his exit is gone. Brady isn't stupid. Gerard is easy to remember with his ink-black hair and beady little eyes. He always looks like he's up to something, and he seems to be everywhere.

"Maybe that's why he looked familiar. I don't know."

Brady's brow furrows in confusion. I school my expression now and slide my fingers across the table to touch Brady's hand. I'm unhappy with myself because I just lied to him.

I never lie, but I can't tell Brady the truth about Gerard. That will just lead to questions and more information, and before I know it, he'll know he just slept with a billionaire.

The longer I can keep my wealth from him, the better. My family's money isn't a factor in our relationship, and I don't want it to be. Besides, I've kept it a secret for this long. I can't exactly bring it up now in conversation. I've never had to tell anyone about my wealth before. It's something that people know about me before they even meet me in person.

"Just look at you two. Don't you look cozy?" Mrs. Tisdale approaches our table, smiling from ear to ear. "I told Mel after dinner at Mayfair last week that I sure hoped you two would hit it off."

"Thank you, Mrs. Tisdale. It's lovely to see you again."

I stand to greet her. In true Davidson fashion, she pulls me to her for a warm hug. She hugs Brady as well.

"I didn't mean to interrupt your time together. I had to pop in to get some treats for our book club meeting this afternoon. Normally, I'd bake something for us to share, but with the holidays and all, I'm baked out. How's your mother doing, Brady? I heard she wasn't feeling well. Will she be in the hospital for long?"

"She should get out today. We were just about to head there now to see how she's doing this morning."

"Please let your parents know we're thinking about them. Goodbye now."

And just like that, Maybelle whirls away to get in line. Her visit was just what I needed to distract Brady from our conversation. I study him, but he gives me no sign that he wants to pick it up where we left off. Thank goodness.

I pop the last bit of baguette into my mouth.

"Ready to go? I'm anxious to see your mom."

Chapter Twenty-Five

Brady

I take Viv's hand in mine again as we walk back to Mayfair to get my van. Leslie's is a block away from Mayfair. The hospital is too far to walk after the night we had together. I still can't believe Viv was going to walk there to see us last night.

For the first time in a long time, I'm happy. Mom is recovering, Mayfair is a success, and I spent an incredible night with a beautiful woman. Now, if I can just not think too much and screw everything up, I could be happy for a while.

But I can't stop thinking about Viv's reaction to the man we saw this morning. She can't continue to claim she doesn't know him. The look she gave him says otherwise. Not only does she obviously know him, she clearly doesn't like him.

But how does she even know him?

The man isn't a local. Did the two of them have some run-in? Maybe he hit on Viv, and she blew him off? If he's bothering her, I could intervene. But Viv must not want my help since she claims not to know him at all. This situation doesn't help my trust issues.

I try not to let my doubts show. No, *doubt* is too strong a word. There's no doubt I like Viv very much. My thoughts are more akin to worries. Another heartbreak is not what I need right now. I'm clearly supposed to be with Viv, or it wouldn't feel this good to be here with her.

"Are you ready for this?" I ask before we head into Mom's hospital room.

"Why do you ask that whenever we're about to see your family? They're wonderful. What do I have to be afraid of?"

I raise our clasped hands. "There will be much rejoicing. Prepare yourself."

She smiles.

"I think I can handle it."

"I'm not sure I can. Let's get this over with."

Mom's eyes meet mine and then Viv's and then lock onto our clasped hands. A giggle erupts despite her tired look. She claps her hands together.

"This is just the news I needed today. Hello, Viv. Hi, sweetheart. It's so good to see you *both* today."

Kate sits in the corner of the room wearing a satisfied grin on her face.

"Don't you need to go open a store or something?"

She stands. "I do. I was just leaving, actually. Nice to see you big brother and very nice to see you, Viv." Kate backs out of the room, still wearing that stupid grin. A sister can be such a pain in the ass. I turn my attention back to Mom.

"How are you feeling this morning?"

"I feel fine. They didn't need to keep me here overnight just because I was feeling a little under the weather. It's the holidays, for goodness sake. 'Tis the season for stress and sleep deprivation."

Dad walks in and hands Mom a cup of tea. His gaze moves to our clasped hands, but in true Dad-fashion, he doesn't say a word.

"I ran into Dr. Hanover outside. He'll be in soon to examine you, but he thinks you'll be able to go home later this morning. Your fever's gone, and that's what they were worried about the most."

"Knock-knock." Granny Simms and Kennedy walk into the room. Granny takes one look at me and Viv and says, "I knew you two would hit it off. Didn't I tell you, Kennedy?"

Viv blushes an uncomfortable shade of red. Doesn't this woman have a filter? Honestly.

It's for Mom's sake alone that I don't ask Granny to knock it off. Instead, I take a deep breath, count to ten, and excuse Viv and myself. Mom has way more visitors than she needs, and I've had enough family time for one day.

❖❖❖

I haven't had a woman in my house who isn't family since Jamie. Crap, Jamie was a huge disaster. Sure, she was a criminal, but a big part of the disappointment comes down to the fact that she kept secrets from me. Just like Viv is keeping things from me. She still hasn't told me about her family money. What else is she keeping from me?

I swallow hard in an effort to shove all the insecurity down as well. Viv is the most fantastic woman I've ever known. She's cultured, beautiful, and being with her brings sensations to my body that I've never thought possible.

And she's only in town temporarily.

My feelings all day have alternated between how much more I want to know about Viv and how much she has yet to tell me about herself. Yes, they are sort of the same thing, but somehow, what she's withholding from me seems more vast than what she's disclosed.

"Your house is homier than I would have expected for a bachelor." Viv looks at me now with wide, smiling eyes. "Sure you have the big television and leather sofa, like you said, but you also have personal photos and throw pillows."

"The stupid pillows were Kate's doing. The

pillows spend more time on the floor than on the couch. She also insisted I paint the walls this light gray color. I admit that it looks nice, but they looked fine when they were white."

"Kate really does have a good eye for design. She's made your house look really cozy."

Cozy. That's like code for small. Yes, my house is small, but so what? It's the perfect size for one person or a small family. Plus, it's all mine.

"Yeah. Well I guess it isn't as big as *some* houses, but I like it."

Viv closes the distance between us and takes my hand. "Brady, I meant it as a compliment. Your house is soft and comfortable, a quality difficult to achieve in a large home. I really do like it. This living room and your dining room are just the right size. Plus, you do have those thick, wooden moldings you mentioned."

I invited Viv here after work tonight because I'm dying to be with her again. I can't stop thinking about being with her last night, and I can't breathe without remembering the scent of her skin. Now that work is over and we have a chance to be together again, I'm sabotaging myself by thinking of her secrets. Those thoughts aren't going to get me what I want.

And what I want is Viv.

She tilts her head up. Her lashes flutter as she closes her eyes and then opens them again. She leans forward and kisses me. It feels as if my whole body sighs as her lips touch mine. I feel the smile on her lips as she breaks our kiss.

"Want to show me how cozy your bedroom is?"

"Absolutely."

Chapter Twenty-Six

Viv

Warmth. That's my first thought upon waking up in Brady's bed. My back is to him. Brady's arm is draped protectively over me. I sigh to myself as I take it all in.

I don't want to go home.

The words come as a flash of light, as if my brain screams them out to make me hear them. The truth has been there niggling in my mind for days. I've done my best to ignore the creeping thoughts, but I can put them off no longer.

I slide out of bed, wrap myself in one of Brady's flannel shirts, and head downstairs. Brady didn't seem to like it when I used the word *cozy* to describe his home, but it truly is. Besides the fact that what I said is completely accurate, I meant it as a compliment. The rooms aren't large, but they're big enough.

The first floor has a combination living and dining area. Brady has the typical leather man-couch and large-screen television. He also has a matching love seat and matching tables and lamps.

The dining area holds an oblong table with six matching chairs. The kitchen is admittedly pretty plain, but the yellow curtains that hang over the window add a pop of color. The short hallway past the kitchen connects to a small laundry room and an office with a very messy desk. Papers are piled in the work area beside a computer beside a framed photo of Brady and Hunter holding a very large fish.

I sigh to myself and return to the kitchen to make coffee. Fortunately, the coffee pot is an easy one to figure out, and coffee begins brewing. I'm not the best cook, but despite the fact that I was born with a silver spoon in my mouth, I can make a few dishes.

The morning air carries a heavy chill, especially on my bare legs. I open the large blinds that cover Brady's sliding glass door and see exactly why. Brady's deck and small fenced-in yard and everything beyond is covered in a thin layer of white.

I don't want to go home. The thought slams into me again, demanding to be dealt with. With a heavy sigh, I make my way to the couch, fold my legs underneath me, and pull a blanket over my lap. I pick up my purse from the coffee table and take out my antique compact. I run my fingers over the design as I have a thousand times. The metal feels cold against my fingers.

What am I going to do?

Grandmother isn't the kind of person who takes *no* for an answer. Actually, that's not true. No one tells Grandmother *no* in the first place. My family allows her to wield her power over them. Everyone does. Because they want Grandmother's money.

The thing is, I don't need Grandmother's money anymore. I have a job. It's a temporary job, of course, but I've proven to myself that I can make money. Can I make enough to survive on my own?

I look down again at the compact and the fairy couple embossed in the center. I always imagined the fairy gentleman to be whispering sweet words into the ear of the woman he loves, as if nothing could ever keep them apart. It's a silly pastime, indulging in these fantasies. Yet, something inside me won't give up on them.

I told myself that I embarked on this mission to find myself. Truthfully, I was hoping and praying for fate to intervene in my life and take me down a different path, my own path, not the one Grandmother had made for me. Now, I'm at a crossroads. Do I go back home as I promised and live the life I've always been told I was destined to live? Or do I stand and fight for the life I want?

I don't want fake friends and fundraisers. I want genuine relationships and holidays with family who expect nothing more from me than my love. I've proven I can get this far. I have a temporary job and a temporary place to live.

I can make a life for myself.

If I can't make enough working as a waitress, maybe I can sell some of my paintings. Or maybe I can get some work painting murals. Hope for the future bubbles up inside me. Can I really do this? Kate posted photos of my Eiffel Tower mural on her blog, and it got a lot of positive feedback. Maybe I really can make money painting.

This little life I've made for myself here in Davidson is so much better than what I have with my family at Manningsgate. I don't want to live in that big house with the grounds and servants. I would miss Rose, of course, but I know she will always be a part of my life.

Maybe I could pay Brady rent if he'll allow me to stay in my little apartment above Mayfair. Truthfully, I want to stay in town with Brady. I want to know him better. I want to know if the spark I've felt inside of me since I met him will continue to grow. I will never know that if I go home. I will never know what could have been. I will only know late nights alone. I will always wonder what people want from me.

It's settled. I'm staying.

My cheeks immediately flush at the thought. This is the right decision, but I have two important jobs to do before I can stay.

First of all, I have to tell Brady about my family. I can't continue to keep secrets from him. It isn't like I'm a murderer or I know someone who is. It's just that my family has money. That's all. He'll likely be happy to hear the news. But then, that's exactly what I'm worried about, isn't it? I don't want Brady to be so happy about the news that he no longer sees me the same way. Either way, I have to find the courage to tell him.

Secondly, there's Grandmother. I have to come clean with her as well; however, it's almost the opposite message. I don't want her money. Grandmother may never understand. All she knows is people groveling to her so that they can have a piece of her. She won't understand my reluctance to accept the gifts she wants to bestow on me. In the end, if giving up my inheritance is what I want, she can't make me take it.

"What's that?"

I look up to see Brady watching me from only a few steps away. I was so caught up in my thoughts that I didn't see him approach. I pull back the blanket to make room for him next to me. He sits on the couch, I cover his lap, and then hold the compact out to him so he can see it clearly.

"This is my most prized possession. It was a gift from my grandmother." I catch my words and correct them. "It's from my *other* grandmother, not the one I've spoken of before." I open it and show him the mirror inside. It's piqued slightly on the edges, but considering it's almost one hundred years old, it's in great condition.

"Tell me about it. Is it worth a lot of money?"

"Not really. It only has sentimental value. My mother's mother gave it to me when I was a little girl. I only saw that set of grandparents three times in my life. I was ten years old the last time I visited. My grandmother gave me this mirror then. She said it belonged to her when she was a teenager, and she always loved it. She passed away only a few months later. I know it sounds silly, but I've always felt like the fairies on the cover were rooting for me."

Brady's blue eyes soften. He wraps his arm around my shoulders.

"That doesn't sound silly at all."

This is the perfect moment to tell Brady everything. I could explain to him how this compact was a treasured possession of my grandmother who had no money, and I've loved it more than anything given to me by my other grandmother, who can afford to give me anything my heart desires.

I open my mouth, but the words don't come. Brady turns his head and looks at me as if he knows I'm trying to speak to him, maybe even expects to be told something important. *Nothing*.

I can't do this. I want Brady to know, but I can't stand the thought of him changing his feelings for me. The words will come to me when the time is right. I snuggle into Brady and breathe in his faint sandalwood scent. This is where I want to be, and I don't want anything to get in the way.

❖❖❖

It seems the only one who's surprised about Brady and me as a couple is Brady. I don't know that he really was all that surprised, but he did fight the idea for longer than he should have. I'm sure it's because I'm keeping secrets, and he knows it.

It's been almost two days since I declared to myself that I had to tell Brady about my wealth. Yet, somehow, I can't find the words. I don't want what we have to end even though I know we can't go much further in our relationship without total honestly.

Am I just hoping for the truth to come out on its own? Maybe. In this age of the Internet and social media, you'd think someone would have found me by now. Miraculously, no one here in Virginia seems to know about my family's money yet. While part of me appreciates that the secret's safe, another part of me wishes Brady would find out without me having to tell him.

I know I should just break down and tell him myself. We've been together the past three nights. I just can't seem to get the words out. The biggest reason is that I don't want to be treated differently. I really like how Brady is with me right now. I don't want to blow it. I also don't know how I could tell him without him wondering why I didn't tell him in the first place.

Maybe if I explained it very carefully he would understand.

I do appreciate that he isn't trying to keep what's happening between the two of us a secret. Brady doesn't hold my hand while we're at work or anything that obvious, but everyone who works at Mayfair knows we're a couple. Of course, it could be because this is such a small town, and everyone seems to know everything. So why haven't they figured out about me yet?

"You okay?"

Meg walks into the storage room where I came to put away some unused clean linens. I did do that, but now, I find myself standing by the door in a trance.

"Sorry. I'm fine."

"You look like you have a lot on your mind."

A heavy sigh escapes. "I guess I do."

"Do you need to talk to someone about it?"

Do I? It would sure feel good to get another opinion.

"I have something I need to tell Brady." Meg shows no reaction, so I continue. "It isn't a bad thing, but it is something about me he should know. I've never had to tell people because at home, everyone knows already." I wrinkle my nose and shake my head. "You know, this isn't really working, is it?"

"Not really, but let me say this. I came to

Davidson almost a year ago, and I brought a few whopper secrets with me. I couldn't tell Tyler. I couldn't tell anyone. They were doozies, too, trust me. Brady didn't judge me, and he didn't demand that I tell him what I was hiding. Brady was very understanding about everything."

"Was that before or after this Jamie person ripped his heart out?"

Meg smiles, puts her hand on my shoulder, and squeezes. "It was after, but let's be clear about Jamie. From everything I've heard about it, Brady didn't love Jamie. The heartbreak, if you want to call it that, was brought about because he trusted her and she squashed him so brutally."

"Really?"

"For sure, and although I wasn't here to see how Brady looked at Jamie, I would be surprised if he looked at her the same way he looks at you. The man has it bad."

"I sure hope so."

And I hope Brady likes me after I tell him the truth.

Chapter Twenty-Seven

Brady

I thought we'd be more comfortable together at my house than here in this little apartment. I was wrong. Viv and I spent the last two nights at my place, and while it was phenomenal, it wasn't like being here. Maybe it's simply because this is where we first made love. Maybe it's because this tiny place is all the space we need to be together. Who knows?

Viv still hasn't told me about her wealth. She has shared personal information, but she doesn't yet trust me to know about her money. Does she think I might treat her differently? Does she think I might stay with her because of her money? I shake my head in an effort to dislodge the anger that begins to congeal in the pit of my stomach. I don't want to be upset with Viv.

My eyes are drawn to the big window that overlooks the General Store. I walk over to it and look out into the morning light. I concentrate and try to see what Viv looks at when she studies something she wants to paint.

I've seen the General Store my entire life. My parents brought Kate and me there almost every day when we were kids. I worked there as a teenager, and I've walked and driven past the place countless times.

Seeing Viv's painting made me feel like I've never really seen it at all. Viv somehow captured not only the look of the place but details I never noticed before.

There's a pattern in the bricks on the corners of the building. I know that, but before I saw the visual on the canvas, I'm not sure I could have described it in detail. More than the physical look of the place, Viv somehow managed to capture the warmth of the store. Viv is more talented than she realizes.

A few cars wait at the red light at the intersection, but the street is empty of pedestrians except for one man across the street. It's before nine o'clock, and nothing downtown is open yet, so the lack of foot traffic isn't surprising. What is out of the ordinary is the lone man who sits on a bench in front of the general store reading a newspaper in weather this cold. The temperature's in the thirties at least and way too cold for a casual moment outside.

As if he can feel my gaze, he looks up at the window. Well shit. I know exactly who that is—it's the man we saw at the diner and Leslie's.

The man nods his head and returns to reading his newspaper.

What. The. Hell?

Was Viv lying when she said she didn't know him? Is this man stalking her?

There's only one way to find out.

I tiptoe back into the bedroom to check on Viv. She's still sleeping like a baby. I grab my pants, shirt, and shoes and quietly return to the living area before dressing as quickly as I can.

I take a quick glance and confirm the man's still sitting in the same spot. I didn't scare him away with my look. *Good.* I quickly slip on my coat and head outside.

The cold air shocks my lungs with my first breath. This isn't the kind of morning when you relax outside with a newspaper.

The mystery man stands as I approach. He folds his newspaper carefully and lays it on the bench where he'd just been sitting.

"What can I do you for, Mr. Richardson?"

"You know who I am?"

"I do. I think it's time we both stopped playing games."

"Who are you?"

"My name is Gerard Billings. I've been retained

by Ms. Prescott's grandmother to keep an eye on her."

"Why?"

"Not that it's any of your business, but I assume Mrs. Prescott is extremely concerned about her granddaughter's safety. You do know who Ms. Prescott is, don't you? You know she's loaded?"

Alarm bells go off in my head. What is happening here?

"I know Viv has money, but I don't care about that."

"Then you must not know how much Ms. Prescott is worth. I haven't met anyone in her acquaintance who has your nonchalance about her wealth. It's a mind-boggling number."

"What is your job here, exactly?"

"Oh, I just keep an eye on Ms. Prescott and report her location and activities to Mrs. Prescott and her staff."

Her staff?

Geez, maybe it is mind-boggling wealth. Honestly, I wish Viv didn't have money. Then she wouldn't have kept it from me. Viv still hasn't told me about that part of her life, despite the incredible nights we've spent together.

"Does Vivienne know you're here watching her?"

"She does. She's asked me to leave, but seeing as I don't actually work for her, I can't do that."

"What will it take to get you to go away?"

"Not gonna happen. You need to get with the

program here. The woman you just spent the night with can make your financial dreams come true. You can open a chain of your precious Mayfair restaurants in locations all over the country."

"I don't want to do that, and I don't want any of Vivienne's money."

"Look, I'm only trying to help you realize the gift you've been given."

"You stay away from Viv, and you stay away from me."

Like the mature adult I am, I stomp away. I need to talk to Hunter about this guy, but first I need breakfast. I walk to Leslie's. After the night we had together, I'd prefer the Super Duper Breakfast from Minnie's, but I settle for a ham, egg, and swiss on a croissant.

Chapter Twenty-Eight

Viv

I rub my eyes and hope against hope that what I'm seeing out the window isn't happening.

Brady's speaking with Gerard.

This is not good.

I slither to the side of the window and peek down at the two of them. Is Gerard interrogating Brady for Grandmother's sake? Did Brady notice Gerard and question him? Goodness knows we've seen Gerard enough times around town for Brady to become suspicious. My mind spins with the possibilities.

If the two of them were up to no good together, they certainly wouldn't speak to each other in plain sight. The thought lifts my spirits a little. Brady cares about me. I know it. He wouldn't do anything to hurt me.

⁂

Brady knocks on the door and walks inside without waiting for me to open it. He gives me a huge smile before plopping down on the couch next to me. He sets his breakfast offering on the table beside my coffee cup.

My feelings of starvation from only moments ago have subsided. I can't eat at a time like this. How can I be sure Brady's worthy of my trust?

He can't know about the money. How would he know?

Brady could have checked me out. A simple internet search would show enough, although he's given no indication of knowing.

Maybe it was in the little things he surely must have noticed. He did show surprise about the bottle of Opus One we shared. Maybe there were other signs he picked up on.

Maybe this is all in my head. Brady's a friendly guy. Maybe he was simply speaking with Gerard as a welcoming citizen of Davidson. The people here in this town are excessively friendly.

"Aren't you hungry? I'm starving."

The fact that Brady's breakfast sandwich is half-eaten already backs up his statement. I look down at mine.

"It looks delicious. Thank you for going out into the cold to bring me breakfast."

"How do you know? You haven't even unwrapped it yet."

"I was just going by the look of yours."

I pick up the sandwich, unwrap it, and then place it on top of the waxy paper.

"Did you see anyone while you were out?"

"I saw a couple people I know at Leslie's."

"Anyone I might know?"

"I don't think so. I saw a guy I went to high school with and a friend of Mom's. That's about it." Brady looks away from me as he finishes his sentence.

He's lying.

Years of practice at keeping my expression schooled is all that keeps me together in this moment. I will myself to calm down.

Maybe Brady has a perfectly good reason for not telling me about his conversation with Gerard. Gerard is nosey. It's possible he instigated the conversation with Brady. Maybe he made up a question to ask Brady to get him talking.

I can't imagine what Gerard would get out of the conversation. It's impossible to imagine he would ask Brady a personal question. Brady would have mentioned something out of the ordinary.

"Viv, are you okay, sweetheart? You look a little green."

He called me *sweetheart*.

He also said I look sick.

"I think I need to rest today. We've been spending a lot of time together in the last few days. I need to energize for tonight."

A long nap was exactly what I needed to get my head on straight. The exchange I witnessed this morning between Gerard and Brady was nothing more than Gerard's way of talking to my *sweetheart*. Brady used that term for me this morning, so it's fitting that I use it for him as well.

Brady didn't mention the conversation with Gerard because it was of no consequence.

Maybe Grandmother is pushing Gerard to learn more about Brady. Of course, with Grandmother's resources, she could easily do a background check on him and learn everything there is to know. I can't believe she isn't here to check him out herself. When Rose called the other day, I braced myself for just that, but Grandmother didn't come.

I don't want to go home, not yet, and probably not ever. I'm not ready to say I want to stay here in Davidson forever. I would only like to have the freedom to stay here longer, maybe even as long as I need to be here to let fate finish its work.

Speaking of work, the New Year's Eve schedule tonight at Mayfair will be more fun than usual. The restaurant is open for business, but Brady and Meg have ensured all the reservations after eight o'clock are taken by family and friends of their staff. Hunter and Kate will be here, and so will Meg's husband, Tyler, and their friend, Bryce.

Kate smiles at me from across the dining room and walks towards me, greeting some of the guests along the way. She wears a sapphire blue crepe shift that looks stunning on her, even with her little pooch of a baby bump. She's stunning with her red hair pulled back in a loose chignon. She hugs me hello.

"Brady isn't going to make you wear this uniform all night, is he?"

I laugh. "No, actually. The last of my guests just left, and I was about to go upstairs and change. Would you like to help me?"

"Absolutely."

"Champagne?"

Brady hands me a stemmed glass, and I take it. I secretly hope it's the good stuff, even though I've made up my mind to try not be a snob about that kind of thing anymore. I can't be if I'm going to be making it on my own.

"You can have this, dear sis." He presents Kate with a glass filled with liquid a little lighter in color than mine. "The finest vintage of sparkling grape juice I could find. I bought two bottles just for you."

Kate and I clink our glasses, and I take a sip. My eyes meet Brady's. He's now opened Mayfair's third bottle of Dom. We share a small knowing smile.

"We'll be right back."

Kate grabs my arm and pulls me toward the kitchen and down the hallway to the stairs that lead up to my little apartment. Funny how I keep thinking of it as my apartment when I don't even pay rent to stay here. This little place feels more like home than anywhere I've ever lived before and certainly more than Manningsgate. I can attribute the homey feel to the people I've met here.

"Will Kennedy be able to make it tonight?"

Kate sighs. "No, they decided to keep Minnie's open until two. Kennedy's working until close. I know she'd love to be here, but she's hoping to make a lot of money tonight."

"She works really hard, doesn't she?"

"Like you wouldn't believe. They lost their parents when they were young. Hunter, Kennedy, and their brother, Justin, have had a long haul of it, but they've all done well. It could have easily gone a different way."

I don't know how things will be between all of us if I leave Davidson, but I'd sure like to take Kennedy with me to France this summer. I would love to help her realize her dream of seeing the Eiffel Tower.

We enter my little apartment. Kate sits down on one of the bar stools and looks around the room.

"Now that the holidays are about over, we need to get this room painted. I'm feeling like green is a good color. What do you think?"

I'm not sure I'll be here long enough to enjoy it. I do not vocalize my thoughts. I don't want to bring down the mood with my negativity.

"What about Granny and Frank? Will they be here tonight?"

"Oh, don't get me started on those two."

"What do you mean?"

"Hunter and I just left them unsupervised at bingo."

"What does that mean?"

"Granny plays bingo every Saturday night. They weren't able to have it last week because Saturday fell on Christmas day. To make up for it, they're going all out tonight. She and Frank are completely decked out, and Granny has promised to be on her best behavior."

"You don't believe her?"

Kate laughs. "I don't think the woman can help herself. It probably would help if she didn't bring a flask of bourbon with her and speak her mind every chance she gets, but bless her heart, Granny seems to be a magnet for trouble."

"She's a handful, isn't she?"

"She is. Hunter doesn't want to spend his New Year's babysitting, but he's nervous that she's there alone."

"She has Frank."

"Frank doesn't get into trouble, but he also doesn't stop Granny from causing a fuss. He just shakes his head and lets her do whatever she wants. Hunter's called in a couple favors with a few friends who are there tonight at the fire station. Fingers crossed, the evening will go well."

"I'm sure it will be fine. I'm going to change quickly. I'll be right back."

I walk into my little bedroom and take a look at the dress I left hanging on the bathroom door. I can only imagine that Rose packed it for this very occasion. It's possible she was covering my bases, but even I'm surprised I have a use for a dress this fancy.

It's made of emerald green silk. The cut is very flattering on me, at least it was when I bought it last spring. I haven't yet had a chance to wear it. The best thing about this dress is that I bought it on a rare shopping trip with just Mom. Mom and I didn't always have a great mother-daughter relationship, but we had a great time that day and vowed to try to do it more often. It was the last time we spent alone together before the accident. It was a happy day, and tonight is a happy night. It's silly, but I feel somehow like Rose knew this moment would come.

I wish Grandmother would have packed my suitcase for me and sent it herself. There's no point in having thoughts of Grandmother doing those endearing grandma kinds of things. It just isn't in her nature.

It's funny, thinking of Granny Simms getting into trouble when left on her own. My own grandmother avoids trouble in any way she can. She manipulates and often says things she doesn't mean to your face but then deals with you strategically behind your back. She manipulates people and situations for her own good or the good of those she loves.

Grandmother rarely speaks of anything that didn't go her way. She wants everyone to think her life is always perfectly wonderful. Contrast that with Granny, who seems to tell you exactly what she's thinking whether you want to hear it or not. I've already heard more talk of Granny's and Frank's sex life than I want to, but at least her honesty is refreshing. I can't deny that.

I quickly slip into my dress and touch up my makeup. I don't want to be up here pining over the way I want things to be. I want to be downstairs with Brady, enjoying his company for as long as I can.

"Ready to go back downstairs?"

Kate's eyes widen as she stands. "Holy cow. You look fabulous. Brady's going to flip out."

"Do you think so?"

"He really likes you, you know."

"I hope so, because the feeling's mutual."

Kate and I walk back downstairs, much more carefully now that I'm taking the stairs in my silver strappy heels. Brady meets us at the door to the kitchen. I smile at the sight of his chin as it practically drops to the floor. This is exactly the reaction I was hoping for. Thank you, Rose.

Brady takes my hand and pulls me back into the hall, away from the crowded kitchen. His hands bracket my chin as his lips find mine. His kiss is a promise of more to come later.

"Do you think anyone would miss us if we went upstairs?"

"Probably. You are the owner."

"I suddenly can't wait for closing. From now on, this is your new uniform. I can't believe I made you wear that frumpy tux when you had this dress hanging in your closet. You're smart, you know good wine, and you look like this in a dress. How did I get so lucky?"

A knot of emotion wells up in my throat. I swallow with no relief.

"I tried unsuccessfully to get you to stay in Davidson that first night you worked here and I walked you back to the inn. Do I have any chance in convincing you to stay? I don't want you to go."

The truth hits me hard. I've known it almost since I set my foot in this town, but I ignored it.

I can't go home. I no longer want to live my life for other people. I want to live my life for me and for Brady.

I love him.

I have to come clean and tell Brady everything. Tonight, when we're alone, I'm going to do just that. He needs to know about the money, and he needs to know why Gerard is following me around.

"Brady, you need to come out now. Rhonda's here." Meg speaks the words into the hallway, but she does so from the kitchen.

"I'll be right there," he replies. He smiles again

and kisses me on the cheek.

He takes my hand and pulls me with him into the kitchen. A woman I can only assume is Rhonda stands in the middle of a small crowd. She looks to be in her late forties or maybe even fifty. She has dark, curly hair that falls to her shoulders and wide blue eyes. She smiles when she sees us.

"You must be Vivienne." I return her smile and hold out my free hand for a handshake. "I can't thank you enough for filling in for me while I've been out."

"I was happy to do it."

Rhonda can have no idea how happy being here has made me, although maybe she does because her knowing smile makes me think otherwise.

Kate puts her arm around me and squeezes my shoulder.

"There you are. Why on earth are you standing in the kitchen?"

It can't be.

I turn slowly towards the doorway, hoping my ears have deceived me. They haven't. I practically feel the blood drain from my head to my toes. I take a step to the side to steady myself. Brady grabs my elbow.

"What are you doing here?" I manage to form the words despite my shock.

Brady looks from me to Henry. Henry waltzes into the Mayfair kitchen, his nose held high in the air.

"We planned to announce our engagement tonight. I decided if you can't come home for our big moment, then I'll come here."

"You're engaged?"

Two words. Brady speaks only these two words, and I know I've done him in.

I try to form the words to tell Brady the truth. I'd just decided to tell Brady everything, including everything there is to know about Henry. I hadn't planned on Brady learning about my so-called *engagement* in front of his friends and family. I have to tell Brady the truth, that there isn't a real engagement. It's a family arrangement and nothing more. Brady needs to know I decided two months ago that I'm not marrying Henry.

Brady needs to know a lot of things I should have told him in the beginning. Holding out on him seems silly now. He's not the kind of man who'd want my money. I open my mouth, but the words do not exit.

"Well, not technically. It's just a formality though at this point. Right, sweetheart?"

Sweetheart.

Of all the endearments Henry could have chosen, why did he have to pick that one? It sounded so much better when Brady said it.

"Is this true?"

Brady's found his voice, the hurt replaced with anger. His eyes shine with it.

"Not exactly. It's not like it sounds. Will you let me explain?"

Brady stands taller and balls his fists at his sides. "I asked you if you were engaged. Remember when you told me you weren't? And now your fiancé shows up on the night when I was going to tell you I love you. Do you think because you're loaded you can just use people for your enjoyment and then throw them away? Well, you can't use me."

"Wait. How did you know about the money?" The truth crashes down on me like a tidal wave. "You knew all along, didn't you?"

"Almost." No. It can't be true. "I couldn't let you work at Mayfair without knowing something about you."

Tears fall steadily now. The betrayal works through my soul.

"You knew all along. I trusted you, and you were after my money the whole time."

"I don't want your money."

"Ha. Of course you do. I saw you talking with Gerard this morning. Is he in on the scam, too?"

"I asked you about Gerard when we were at Leslie's the other day, and you told me you didn't know him."

"You lied to me about Gerard as well. Was everything a lie?"

Brady and I stand face to face. His words are laced with anger and contempt. Mine spring forth between bouts of tears. "You know what I want from you?" Three heartbeats practically rattle my ribs as I wait for Brady's response. "Nothing."

Without another word, Brady turns and walks out of the room. The back door of the restaurant slams closed. My tears are the only other sounds. At some point, Meg stopped cooking. She stares at me open-mouthed from behind the island.

Kate, Hunter, and my Mayfair co-workers stare at us in complete shock from where they still maintain their positions around Rhonda, whose mouth is practically on the floor.

Henry smiles. "Well, that was entertaining. Who do I see about a drink?"

"You are such an ass."

Henry shakes his head. A creepy smile forms on his face. "Your lover is working to scam you out of your family money, and I'm the ass? When we get married, you'll need to choose your *relationships* more carefully. I don't care who you sleep with, but I'll be damned if they can have a dime of my money."

I point my finger at Henry's face and stand as tall as I can. He still has several inches on me.

"Let me be perfectly clear. I am not marrying you. How dare you come in here and ruin the best thing that has ever happened in my life?"

"Your grandmother believes otherwise."

"I don't care if it's Grandmother's dying wish. I will never marry you. Now get the hell out of here."

Henry smiles. "Your grandmother is only a phone call away. I will be seeing you again soon, and I won't forgive you easily."

There's no arguing with the man. I no longer care what Grandmother wishes for me. I'm done with that life. Kate steps to me and puts her hand on my shoulder. "Forget this guy. You need to talk with Brady."

"Am I too late?"

"Brady loves you. He just admitted it. Go get him."

I turn on my heels and head out the back door.

Chapter Twenty-Nine

Brady

"Her fiancé!" I scream the words into the cold night and continue my walk down Cherry Street. I don't know where I'm going, but I do know I have to put some distance between me and Viv's asshole fiancé. "She has a fucking fiancé!" My mind is spinning at the meaning of the word. Impossible. Viv told me she's never been engaged, and I believed her. I even believed her when she said she didn't know Gerard. Maybe not immediately, but I talked myself into believing her, even with all the evidence to the contrary. I am such a gullible idiot.

Now what the hell am I supposed to do? Never get married? Never have love?

All that talk about fate and trusting fate. I bought Vivienne's crap when all she was looking for was a quick fling before getting married. Is it my fate to fall in love with women who just want to use me? You know what, fate? Fuck you.

I stop and take a deep breath. The cold air stings my lungs. Just great. I left without a coat. Although my anger fueled me for two blocks, the cold almost-January air has won. With a huge sigh, I turn around and head back towards Mayfair. Fortunately, my keys are in my pocket. Hopefully, I can make it to my van and get the hell out of there before I have to speak with anyone.

There's only one place I care to be at this moment. Only one place where I'm guaranteed to be away from any and all New Year's celebrations. The cabin. It's far enough into the mountains to avoid hearing any partying, whooping, and hollering, and there's an almost-full bottle of tequila in the kitchen cabinet that has my name written all over it.

Looks like that bottle of tequila is going to have to wait. Viv stands at the corner of Main and Cherry Streets as if waiting for me. She walks towards me. She, like me, has no winter coat, but at least I have a suit jacket. She wears only that fantastic dress that only moments ago I was appreciating in the cramped back hallway of Mayfair.

"What the hell are you doing out here? You're going to catch pneumonia."

Viv's shaking in the cold, despite the fact that she

has her arms hugged tightly to her. Tears fall steadily from her cheeks. I resist the urge to wipe them. I'm not getting sucked in. Never again.

"Henry isn't my fiancé. Not really."

"Then what is he, *really*?"

"He is who Grandmother wants me to marry. That part is true, but we are not engaged, and I decided before I even met you that I would never marry him." Viv keeps her elbows at her sides but brings her hands up to her face to wipe the tears from her cheeks. They are quickly replaced with more. "I did tell you that Grandmother has a plan for my life. Henry is part of her plan. I went on this trip in the hopes of finding what I was missing in my life. What I found was a whole new world where I get to call the shots. I'm not going to let Grandmother run my life. I'm not even going back home.

"I should have told you about the money. I should have told you about Gerard and Henry. I didn't at first because I didn't want to be treated differently. My whole life has been that way. I liked working at Mayfair, and I liked having friends that I knew actually liked me and not my money. The longer time went on, the harder it was to speak of it. I was going to tell you tonight. I'm sorry I wasn't honest about the money from the beginning. I'm sorry I accused you of keeping secrets from me, and I'm sorry I accused you of being in cahoots with Gerard. I will only tell you the truth from now on, and the truth is, Brady, I love you, and I don't want to lose you."

Her wide, beautiful brown eyes show only honesty. Viv isn't lying. She laid out her soul to me just now, and I know that every word of it is true. I remove my suit jacket, wrap it around her shoulders, and pull her into my arms.

When her shivering subsides, I pull back enough to look into her eyes. I bring my hand to her cheek and wipe away the remaining tears.

"I'm sorry I didn't tell you I knew about your family fortune in the first place. I should have, but as time went on, it became harder and harder. I wanted you to confide in me and tell me yourself. I won't make that mistake again. I want to tell you now, Viv, that I love you. I love you for you, whether you're rich or poor. I don't want to run your life, but I do want you to stay here in Davidson. Stay with me."

The corners of Viv's mouth curve up into a small, hopeful smile.

"You really want me to stay?"

"Please don't go home. Don't go anywhere."

Her lips find mine in a soft, warm kiss. She does love me. This time is different. This time is real. This is what fate has been preparing me for all along.

Something cold and wet touches my face. I open my eyes to see snowflakes beginning to fall.

"It's snowing," Viv says with a chuckle.

"Want to celebrate a snowy New Year's Eve at the cabin? I'm thinking naked in front of a warm fire."

She nods. "I can't think of anything better."

Chapter Thirty

Viv

The new year is already shaping up to be the best one of my life. It helps to have awakened in front of a warm fire in the arms of my true love. Maybe that sounds corny and childish, but I know it's the truth. I trusted fate to show me a better life, and fate came through.

My stomach rumbles loudly.

"I'm driving as fast as I can," Brady responds with a chuckle. "Luckily, the road was clear enough to make it down the mountain, or we'd be having chicken noodle soup for breakfast. That was the only thing left in the pantry."

"Minnie's biscuits and gravy are worth the wait.

It's been a long time since I've eaten. We left the party last night before we had a chance to eat dinner."

"For good reason." My stomach flips at the memory of Brady walking out of Mayfair last night. He brings my hand to his lips and kisses it lightly. "I love you, Viv."

I don't think I'll ever grow tired of hearing those words. I smile and look into Brady's warm eyes. "I love you, too."

Brady parks in the small lot at Minnie's and walks around his van to open the door for me. It's like neither of us can stop smiling. I've never felt so light.

I look down at the outfit I'm wearing that consists of Kate's old sweatpants and Brady's sweatshirt. Brady wears his father's sweats and an old flannel shirt. We didn't want to take the time to stop at Brady's house and my apartment to change clothes, and we certainly couldn't wear our dressy clothes from last night.

"Am I dressed okay to go out in public?"

"You're perfect."

Brady brackets my neck with his hands, lowers his head, and brings his lips to mine. His kiss is full of hope and a promise that this is what we'll be doing for the rest of the day and maybe even longer. My body responds immediately with a wish to skip breakfast and go to Mayfair so we can see where this will lead. We can't continue to make out like this in the Minnie's parking lot.

Brady breaks our kiss. His pale blue eyes look back at me with such intensity, and yet they're soft and vulnerable at the same time. Brady trusts me now. He loves me. It's all right there.

"Come on. Let's get you something to eat." He takes my hand and pulls me toward the front door.

Minnie's is fairly busy this morning. There's a buzz of conversation but still plenty of empty seats. Kennedy meets us at the door.

"Didn't you work last night?"

"Until one o'clock, and I came back in at eight this morning. I need all the hours I can get for school and my Paris fund." Kennedy escorts us to a booth and leaves us with menus. I slide into the booth, and Brady slides in next to me. I pick up the menu in front of me, although I'm not sure why. I already know what I'm going to eat. My body will have no issues processing all those calories after the night we had together.

The front door opens again, and Granny enters. She waves and walks over to us.

"I hear you two had quite a night last night."

Brady grimaces. "I don't think I want to know what you heard."

As far as I know, there wasn't much to hear. Brady texted Kate to let her know that we had made up and were okay and to carry on the party without us. Does Granny know about that?

"Let's just say I know things are back on track

with you two. Even if I didn't know there was an incident in the Mayfair kitchen, it's obvious the two of you are in love. I'll just leave it at that."

Kennedy walks up and sets mugs and a small coffee pot on our table.

"I'm sure you two had a fun night. Of course, my night was fun too."

Kennedy groans. "Please, Granny. It's too early in the morning to hear the details of your *fun*."

"Oh quiet, you prude. I was talking about how much fun I had at bingo. I won two hundred dollars." We breathe a collective sigh of relief. "Hey, look, it's Bunny. I'm going to go say hello. You two have a nice breakfast."

Granny walks across the room to speak with her friend. Brady and I settle in. I take my first sip of coffee. I close my eyes and let the warmth of the coffee and this moment wash over me.

"Viv."

Brady speaks my name in a breathy tone. I open my eyes and see his blue eyes now blazing with intensity. He angles his body towards mine and sighs heavily.

"I'm not sure how to say this without seeming like I'm telling you what to do, but at least let me tell you what *I* want." I manage a small nod as my mind races with the possibilities of what he's about to say. Brady doesn't give me time to worry before he speaks. "I meant what I said last night. I don't want you to leave." Brady's shoulders relax a little. His words come faster now. "I know you have a life in Boston and a grandmother whom you feel rules your life. I don't want to be like her. I don't want to tell you what to do. But, I want you to stay here. Work at Mayfair or don't. I won't try to run your life. I just don't want to live mine without you."

Brady slides back out of the booth. Where is he going? He turns back towards me and gets down on one knee.

My breath catches. Can this really mean…?

I slide closer to him as my eyes begin to well up with tears.

"Vivienne, we can take all the time you want to take, although I hope it won't be too long. And I want to let you know that I don't want any of your family's money. I'll sign whatever I need to sign to prove that. I love you. Please be my wife."

Brady's eyes are full of love and hope and show me everything I need to know.

He doesn't want me for my money. I knew he didn't, but still, to hear Brady say those words. A lightness fills me, leaving me almost dizzy with happiness.

"I don't mean to interrupt," Grace says quietly. We both turn to her where she stands to the left of Brady. My mind suddenly remembers that we're in the middle of a crowded diner. For the last several minutes, it felt as if it was only Brady and me. "I thought you might need this." Grace pinches a ring between her fingers and holds it out to Brady. "It's just a loan, but by the looks of things, you could use it." Brady takes the ring and studies it. "Carry on."

Grace's sweet smile grows as she backs away from Brady until she's even with Kennedy and Granny, who stand about five feet away, watching us unabashedly. My gaze meets that of Kennedy first. She's crying. Granny smiles from ear to ear with hunched shoulders and hands folded together like she might be praying. It's completely quiet in the noisy diner as everyone watches the happenings at our table.

The sound of the front door draws my attention.

Grandmother.

She stands in the doorway wearing a cranberry-colored suit and pearls, a look she always sports at home at Manningsgate, but she looks completely out of place here at Minnie's.

My first thought is to run. Funny how seeing my grandmother after six months away brings out the fight-or-flight tendencies in me. I watch as she processes the situation, which is pretty simple to figure out. Brady's down on one knee with a ring in his hand. The surprised expression Grandmother wears turns into a bit of a grimace.

I am not going to let her ruin this moment. I reach out and touch Brady's cheek. His focus returns to me.

"Yes." The word comes out as more of a whisper than anything else, not because I don't want Grandmother to hear my answer. No, it's because of the emotion that fills my throat. I swallow hard and continue, "I love you, Brady."

Tears fill Brady's eyes as he slips the ring on my finger. It's a bit too big, but it's perfect. I'm engaged to Brady. He loves me, and I love him, and Grandmother was too late to stop us, not that I would have let her if she tried.

Brady and I stand. He kisses me quickly and then pulls me to him in a tight embrace as Minnie's erupts in a chorus of cheers and applause. Brady releases me, and I'm immediately hugged by Kennedy, Grace, and then Granny. Brady receives many congratulatory pats on the back as well-wishers come at us from seemingly every direction.

Melinda shouts, "Pie's on the house," and another round of cheers erupts.

Once the small crowd disperses, I see Grandmother, still standing in the same spot, her expression unreadable.

I nod. "I love you," I whisper.

"I love you, too." Brady lowers his head and brushes my cheek lightly with his lips as he whispers the words in my ear.

"Is that her, your Grandmother?" Brady asks softly.

I nod, take Brady's hand in mine, and lead him to greet Grandmother. She's about twenty feet away, and her piercing gaze doesn't leave mine as we cover the distance between us.

"Happy New Year," I say as way of introduction.

"It's such a surprise to see you here." I smile and kiss each of her cheeks softly. "Please allow me to introduce you to my fiancé, Brady Richardson." The word *fiancé* somehow rolls off my tongue effortlessly. I love the sound of it.

Brady offers his hand, and Grandmother takes it for a quick handshake. "It's nice to meet you, Mrs. Prescott. We just sat down for breakfast. Would you like to join us?"

I hold my breath as Grandmother looks around the dining room. Minnie's Diner is a far cry from the country club where she occasionally eats Sunday brunch or grabs a quick breakfast after an early tennis match. This is the land of cholesterol and carbs, two things Grandmother avoids at all costs.

"I will not be required to have pie for breakfast, will I?"

"Only if you wish to," Brady says with a smile. Grandmother smiles—she smiles—and follows us back to our booth. This is the booth where I became engaged only a few moments ago. Now, Grandmother is with us, and she's smiling. How can this be happening? I must be dreaming.

Brady and I sit as we were before. Grandmother sits across from us. She glances down at the laminated menu without picking it up. I take this moment to study her. She looks as put together as always with her St. John's suit. Her steel gray hair is pulled back into a low chignon. It's how she's worn her hair for as long as I can remember. I've rarely seen her with a hair out of place. Grandmother wouldn't leave the house without looking perfectly polished.

Something is different this morning. There are dark patches under her eyes. Sure, she's tried to cover them up with concealer, but they're still clearly there. Has she been that worried about me or something else?

Kennedy approaches our table, carrying a mug and a full pot of coffee. She stops a few feet away and looks at me with questioning eyes as if asking permission to bring us coffee. I give her a quick nod, and she takes the last few steps to our table.

"Good morning, ma'am. Would you like some coffee?"

Grandmother looks up from her perusal of the menu. "Coffee would be lovely. Just black. Thank you." Kennedy places the Minnie's Diner mug in front of Grandmother and fills it to the rim. She takes her time with the task, checking out Grandmother briefly, but spending most of the time looking at me. It occurs to me that Kennedy wants to make sure that I'm okay. I choke back a swell of emotion and manage a small smile. I love it that my new friends care about me so much.

"Grandmother, may I introduce you to Kennedy Simms. Kennedy is just one of the many good friends I've made during my stay here in Davidson."

Grandmother studies Kennedy for a few seconds. She doesn't lay into me about having friends who are waitresses or the fact that I've been working as one myself. She simply says, "Lovely to meet you, Kennedy." It's such a small thing, but I feel a whoosh of relief nonetheless.

Kennedy excuses herself. Grandmother turns her piercing gaze to Brady and me. This is it. She knows I'm engaged to Brady, and she can't be happy with this news. She's wanted me to marry Henry for years.

I haven't known what I wanted for much of my life, but I know now. Sure I've stood up to Grandmother before. I convinced her to let me major in art history in college, and I stayed fast on my determination to set out on a Harley when I really had no business riding the thing. Neither of those moments compare to what I have to say to her now.

I swallow down my anxiety, sit as tall as I can, and take Brady's hand in mine. "I don't want to disappoint you Grandmother, but I won't be coming home with you today." The words come out too fast, spoken in one quick breath. I pause to see Grandmother's reaction. Her face has the same reserved expression she always wears. She likely came to that conclusion on her own when she saw me accept Brady's marriage proposal. I take another deep breath and finish my declaration. "In addition to that, I would like to forfeit my share of the Prescott fortune."

That news does come as a shock. Grandmother's eyes widen. Her jaw falls for a split second before she closes her mouth and begins shaking her head. "Now, now, we should discuss this situation before you make rash statements."

My words are far from rash. Maybe it seems sudden to Grandmother, but I've known for a long time that her money didn't make me happy. Yet, I didn't know how to merge that fact with the reality that everyone around us acted as if her money was vital to life. Fate showed me what I needed and that I can live and be happy without the Prescott fortune.

"I can take care of Viv, and, more than that, she can take care of herself. She's amazing." Brady's tone is firm and reassuring. "I wouldn't want her to give up anything she's due because of me, but we don't need your money to be happy. We only need each other."

Brady's words warm my heart. I feel the moisture in my eyes and do my best to hold it back. Grandmother's never been a fan of tears of any kind. She's always told me they are a sign of weakness. Grandmother takes a slow, thoughtful sip of coffee.

"Is this how you both feel?"

Brady and I nod in unison. It's all I can do to keep my smiles on the inside. This is what I've always dreamed of, a man who loves me for me. I can hardly believe this moment is happening.

Grandmother, of all things, smiles. It isn't a crooked, mischievous smile. It appears to be genuine. She shakes her head and sighs loudly. "This has turned out to be one helluva week."

I'm no longer sure what's happening. I only know that Grandmother doesn't sigh or use phrases like *helluva*.

"Excuse me?" I finally manage to ask.

"In my life I've always done a good job of making things work out like I think they should. That is, until you went away on your voyage of self-discovery." Grandmother's expression turns wistful as she continues. Brady holds onto my hand tighter as if he knows we're about to go on a bumpy ride. "You wouldn't change your mind about the trip. You knew I was against it. I gave you all my usual, subtle and not-so-subtle hints. You were determined."

"I really needed to find myself."

"I know you did. I was angry that you disobeyed me, and I was worried about your safety. A young woman traveling alone in such a manner, especially when you could barely ride on that death trap." She pauses and shudders at the mere thought of it. "I couldn't talk you out of going, so I felt I had no choice but to hire someone to watch over you. They were supposed to watch from a distance. You should have never known they were there, and you didn't until that Gerard gentleman. He came onboard when the man before him had to leave for a family emergency. Gerard is obviously not very good at his job since you spotted him within days. Of course, thanks to Rebecca and your Uncle Patrick, Gerard had different duties to perform than the man who was previously on the job."

"What do you mean?" I don't want to interrupt this story, but I don't want to miss anything either.

"Uncle Patrick and Rebecca conspired to keep you away from Manningsgate."

"Why?" Brady asks first before I can speak the question myself.

"They were trying to get all my money." Grandmother sighs again, more heavily this time, and continues. "Rebecca has worked for me for almost thirty years. I have always treated her with respect and provided her with a place to live and compensated her well. Maybe being around wealth made her believe she should have her share. I'm not sure. She was working with Patrick to get your share of the money."

My jaw drops now.

"How can that be? Uncle Patrick has more money than he can ever spend."

Grandmother nods. "Apparently, that wasn't enough for him and his family. When your parents passed away, and you wanted to go on your little trip, he used his circumstances to try to convince me to disinherit you."

"If Patrick has enough money on his own, what does he gain from disinheriting Viv?"

"More money and security for his family. He knows I have a special place in my heart for you, Vivienne. You have a much better head on your shoulders than your cousins. That's part of the reason why I wanted you to help me with the foundation. Patrick saw that as a threat to his family. You have more of a heart than those vultures. You genuinely care about the people we help. Patrick's family is only about the show."

"Is that why Rebecca wouldn't let me speak with you this past week?"

"It is. I learned that she brought you clothing to make your stay here in Davidson more comfortable. She and Patrick are also the ones responsible for taking your motorcycle. Their time was running out, and since they weren't making any progress with their plan, they were desperate."

"I disapprove of what Uncle Patrick and Rebecca did, but everything has worked out for me. Staying here in Davidson is the best thing that's ever happened to me."

Grandmother reaches for my hand across the table. She squeezes tightly. "I can see that. You have always been different than the rest of the family. I've always known you to be a loving and trusting person. I'm sorry that I pushed you to live your life as I thought it should be lived. I had what I thought was your best interest at heart."

She squeezes Brady's hand with her other hand. "I can see that you're where you need to be."

"Thank you." Brady's voice sounds rough and emotional. I don't dare speak. The tears well up in my eyes now. There's no holding them back.

"However, the circumstances have not worked out very well for me." I look from Brady back to

Grandmother. My question must be written on my face because she answers before I speak. "I've fired Rebecca and disinherited Patrick. Wouldn't Patrick be beside himself to learn that you don't want the money? His plan of keeping you away actually worked."

"I can't believe Uncle Patrick would do that to me." My own family trying to manipulate Grandmother to push me out of the picture. It's unbelievable.

"He seriously thought I would fall for his silly plan. Like I was born yesterday. Please." She pauses for a thoughtful moment and then continues. "Please don't give away your inheritance yet. Let me prove to you that we can be a real family even with gobs of money. I want you in my life, even if you live in this tiny town far away from me. Will you think about it at least?"

"I will. Besides, you aren't far...just a short plane ride away."

Grandmother smiles, lets go of both our hands, and takes another sip of coffee. "The coffee here is really good."

"It is. Wait until you have the biscuits and gravy."

"For breakfast? I thought the idea of pie for breakfast was appalling."

"You've never had biscuits and gravy?"

We look up to see Granny standing next to our table, looking like she's about to burst with excitement. Grace grabs Granny's arm and tries to pull her away.

"Granny, leave them alone."

One look into Granny's hopeful eyes, and I know I can't turn them away.

"Why don't you both join us for breakfast?"

"Grandmother, please meet Grace Richardson, Brady's mother." They share a kind greeting. "This other lovely woman is…Granny, I apologize, but I can't remember your first name."

"Beverly Simms," Granny says proudly as she shakes Grandmother's hand.

"Lovely to meet you, Beverly. You are Brady's grandmother?"

"No. Most people in town just call me Granny."

"She isn't technically my granny, but I like to think that she is."

Brady and Granny share a sweet smile as the two women get settled. Grace pulls a chair up to sit at the end of our table, and Granny scoots into the booth with Grandmother. Kennedy brings two more mugs and pours coffee for us all.

I turn again to Brady. He kisses me again, this time on the cheek. We share a smile.

"You trusted fate with your life, and I'm the one who got everything I ever wanted."

"We both did."

Dear Reader,

I hope you enjoyed *Trusting Fate*. If so, please consider writing an online review. Reviews are very helpful and would be very much appreciated.

If you would like to be notified of upcoming releases, please sign up for my newsletter at www.tamralassiter.com. I'd also love to connect with you on Twitter or Facebook.

Sincerely,

Tamra Lassiter

Acknowledgements

My cousin-in-law, Rhonda Allen, has been extremely supportive to me in my writing efforts. She's been a fan from my very first book and has always helped me spread the word among her friends. More than that, she is an amazing person. Rhonda has endured some very difficult times in her life and through it all has been one of the most uplifting people I have ever met. Her strong faith in God is at the heart of her every being, and she is a beacon of inspiration to all who know her. Thank you, Rhonda, for being you.

Many thanks to my friends and family who are my beta readers. Thanks to Jeri Lassiter, Suzanne Bhattacharya, Anne Newport, June Kuhne, Peggy Lassiter, and Pat Williams.

Special thanks to Mary McGahren for this amazing cover. I love these Role of Fate covers!

Thanks to Jena O'Connor of Practical Proofing, Toni Metcalf, and Mary Featherly for all your help with editing and proofing.

Also by Tamra Lassiter

Other titles in the *Role of Fate* series:

Deciding Fate

Blinding Fate

Creating Fate

Guiding Fate

Romantic Suspense:

No More Regrets

Perfectly Innocent

Something to Lose

I Take Thee to Deceive

Favorable Consequences

Young Adult Fantasy:

The Gifted